How We Move the Air

Also by Garnett Kilberg Cohen:

Fiction

Lost Women, Banished Souls (University of Missouri Press)

Poetry Chapbook

Passion Tour (Finishing Line Press)

How We Move the Air

A collection of linked stories

by Garnett Kilberg Cohen

Mayapple Press 2010

Published by MAYAPPLE PRESS
               408 N. Lincoln St.
               Bay City, MI 48708
               www.mayapplepress.com

ISBN 978-0932412-93-5

ACKNOWLEDGMENTS

I wish to thank the publications where the following stories originally appeared: *TriQuarterly* "Afterlife"; *Crazyhorse* "Second Sight" (winner of the
2004 *Crazyhorse* National Fiction Prize); *The Roanoke Review* "Behind the
Door" (published under the title "The Cure," the story was a runner-up for
the magazine's national fiction prize).

I appreciate the generous support of the Illinois Arts Council and of Co-
lumbia College Chicago (particularly Provost Steven Kapelke; Deborah
Holdstein, Dean of LAS; and Ken Daley, Chair of the Department of
English).

I am especially indebted to the wonderful editors at Mayapple Press, Judith
Kerman, Amee Schmidt, and Matthew Falk, and to those friends, writers,
and relatives who either read early drafts of some or all of the stories in
this collection and offered feedback or provided another form of support
or inspiration: Victoria Anderson, Wendy Bartlo, Rosellen Brown, Tsivia
Cohen, Beverly Donofrio, Stuart Dybek, Sharon Evans, Bill Frederking,
Kim Green, Maggie Kast, Chuck Kinder, Mark Kelly, Jim Kilberg, Sara
Livingston, Susie Rosenthal, Tom Rosenthal, Elizabeth Shepherd, Peggy
Shinner, Bob Snyder, Sharon Solwitz, S.L. Wisenberg.

Gratitude to the multi-talented Audrey Niffenegger who generously
provided use of her etching, "The Lovers," from the *Vanitas Series*, for the
cover of this book, and to Printworks Gallery of Chicago who represents
her. And, finally, another note of thanks to Sara Livingston who took the
author photo.

Cover designed by Judith Kerman. Book designed and typeset by Amee
Schmidt with cover titles in Bleached, story titles in Berlin Sans, and text
in Adobe Caslon Pro.

Contents

...the waves of a sound are an agitation of the air moving steadily forward through the air. The air does not move bodily from place to place with the sound, and the air can support many independent sound waves simultaneously...

—*Van Bergeijk, Pierce, & David,* Waves and the Ear

The dead don't go; they just slip into other people's heads.

—*Penelope Lively,* The Photograph

For Fred

Chicago Tribune

Obituaries
October 17, 1985

Doyle, Jacek (Jake), 30, died at home on October 15. A musician, Doyle is a graduate of the University of Illinois at Chicago, where he also attended graduate school. He is survived by his wife, Yolunda (nee Lobwoski); one daughter, Coco; brother, Daniel; and sister, Catherine. Services to be announced.

Afterlife

You're still dead. I was thinking it as I was driving, listening to some sentimental pop tune from the seventies, a song you would have flipped off before most people had a chance to identify it. (I can still see the endearing twist of your lips that indicated disdain.) I was on my way home from the hairdresser—yes, I color it now, something I promised I would never do—who had just told me she had been diagnosed with a terminal illness. She must have forgotten that she had told me the same thing (albeit a different illness) four years ago when I had first started using her. (People should keep track of whom they tell they're dying and when.) I remember the exchange distinctly because I had wondered if I should continue with her or switch to another stylist before I got too attached. Finally it had seemed too mean to abandon a dying woman without insurance, particularly since I'm such a terrific tipper.

So yesterday, when she delivered this bad news with a quivering lower lip as if it was hard to reveal such a thing, I wanted to say, *but you're still alive four years after the diagnosis of an inoperable brain tumor.* (Of course I never say what I want to say.) And that, circuitous as it may seem, is how I came to the realization in my car. My hairdresser is still alive. And you're still dead. Granted, it has been a much longer time for you.

Last night, I couldn't sleep; my thoughts tore through my mind, thoughts of you, all the things I've wanted to tell you. All night, my brain traveled in a loop so that now, at the first grey-pink light of dawn, I am sitting at the kitchen table in my night gown, writing to you in the hope that by putting my thoughts down on paper I will still the constant drone in my mind and, finally, clear my head.

I have divorced and completed grad school. My daughter, Molly, about the age I was then, lives out on the west coast now.

(You should see her. Beautiful. Tall and dark and lush. Like me, only she knows it and uses it in ways I never could.) I have switched jobs so many times I'd have to write a list to remember them all. While all this has been happening, you have been dead. If you were trying to make a point, it was obviously a mistake. The point lasted a few weeks, months maybe, a year at best. Death much longer.

I think of you most often in the autumn—when the leaves turn and everything seems overgrown, beyond fecundity. But lately, thoughts of you have arrived unexpectedly, and, I must admit, with increasing intensity. The force of these remembrances makes me want to talk to you, clarify what happened.

Did you wonder how I would learn the news? Did you think Yolunda would call and we would grieve together? Everything forgiven on her part? Well, I can tell you—it didn't happen that way. Carlos told me. (You know, the guy you used to buy your pot from. You wouldn't believe how rich he is now! Owns a string of video game rooms and a God-awful *nouveau riche* house, closer into the city, with huge gargoyles perched over the double front doors. When we see each other, we pretend not to know one another. And we don't really. We were different people back then.) Anyway, a couple months after you and I broke up, I called him myself. Michael had already quit smoking dope. You were my only connection. *Too bad about your old man,* Carlos said in that stoned drawl that seemed so sexy back then. *Yeah, well, things end,* I said, thinking he was referring to our break-up, though a little surprised that you would confide in Carlos. *Wow, you are one cold bitch, no wonder he blew his brains out.* I laughed, said *fuck you,* and hung up the phone without making arrangements to pick up the pot. I didn't believe him, thought it was just a crazy-dope-dealer thing to say. I learned the details of your suicide just a few hours later.

Your funeral was held north of the city in the forest preserve, in the dazzling autumn sunshine. You would have liked the sound of the leaves rustling in the trees, the way the bright light illuminated each individual leaf. And you would have been proud of Yolunda. She played her role—the brave widow—with more flair than I would have expected. Decked out in festive colors (Coco, too), Yolunda told the crowd it was to be a celebration of your productive life, not a mourning of your one final desperate act. Everyone you would have wanted showed up. Even that guy, Landers, to whom you lost that last commission to compose a piece for the installation at the cultural center. They wanted you, I heard, but you refused to compromise. Even for five thousand—a lot of money at the time. (I always admired the way you stuck to your aesthetic principles.) About the only person who wasn't at your funeral was Michael. I talked him out of it. He wanted to go, argued that it didn't matter that Yolunda and I had had a fight. After all, he reasoned, the four of us, you and Yolunda and Michael and me, had been friends so long. He stressed the fact that our kids, Molly and Coco, were buddies. (He also said that your mistake was marrying Yolunda, that you would have been better off with someone like me. I didn't tell him that you had been with me. Many times.) I stuck to my guns (pardon the expression) and refused to go, said no, I wouldn't risk upsetting Yolunda, making things harder for her than they already were. He never suspected that I feared what Yolunda might reveal to *him*. Why would he? Michael trusted me. But the second he headed down the street for the train to work, I called Edge and asked her to watch Molly.

I went by myself, wearing the only black outfit I had, an itchy wool suit my mother had given me, without nylons—the weather was exceedingly hot for October. (I have since wondered if you would have done it in May when the daffodils were blooming. Not as many people off themselves these days. They have amazing drugs for depression now! It's a brave new world.) I stood in the back, like the "other woman" in a bad movie, and sweated and scratched and cried. The event was a retrospective of your work. Once the speakers came on, the leaves stopped moving—or seemed to. Both of your two biggest commissions were played, a few soundtracks, and that sweet little chamber piece—I wonder what Yolunda would have done if she had known you wrote it for me? I cried a lot. As I was leaving, I spotted Carlos (standing on the periphery as I had been) and asked if he still had my pot. He said to meet him at his place, so I picked up Molly, swung by Carlos's, then went home and got stoned.

Molly is juggling two guys now, one on the east coast and one on the west. Her job forces her to coast hop a lot. I tell her the game she's playing isn't wise; the guys will be hurt; she'll be hurt; it will all end badly. Michael knows about it too. He disapproves on moral grounds. We don't speak much. His second wife doesn't like it; besides, it's painful for both of us. When we do talk, we try not to get too personal. Yet in a recent, unguarded moment, he said it was my influence that made Molly so bold. Michael never knew about you; I did tell him about the guy after you. So he *thinks* he knows the score. But he only knows what I let him know. Sure, I might have looked brazen (even to you, I bet), but that wasn't the case. If Molly does take after me, it isn't boldness—it's fear: fear of being left alone, fear of making the wrong decision, fear of not having enough, fear of disappointing someone. Though Michael has the cause of my actions wrong, I do wonder just how responsible I am for Molly's behavior. Remember those times I brought her to your studio when we thought she was too young to catch on, those times she saw us kiss, our thirsty mouths finding it so hard to separate? Maybe being exposed to all that had some kind of subliminal, postponed effect.

It was better when Molly wasn't there, when Edge would watch her so I could come alone. I loved that little building, encased in all those fiercely clinging vines, the way it was almost hidden at the back of your overgrown yard. Both our spouses at work. Coco in day care. It seemed like we were the only people alive in a sea made of instruments and equipment and soundboards and music, floating on the musty mattress in the center of the studio. We would smoke that pungent pot you got from Carlos. (Remember the tape you made of seeds popping over seeds popping over seeds popping, a symphony of grass, with the intention of getting a refund?) I loved to listen to you talk about music, how noise *made* an environment but most people didn't even recognize that what they were hearing contributed to how they felt. Then we would make love on that damp mattress (I still get excited from the smell of must), amidst all your sounds and scents. Our lovemaking had a long afterlife. Hours later, my fingertips and toes still tingled and my legs felt boneless. When I rode my bike home it seemed like music came from everything: the trees, the clouds, the smoke spurt, spurt, spurting from chimneys. We lost track of time so often that I'm surprised it took Yolunda so long to catch us. Though technically, I suppose, we were never really caught. She simply spotted me leaving the studio, wading knee-deep in the middle of your overgrown lawn.

"I thought you were my friend!" she screamed.

I wanted to say, *I am your friend. What does the fact that I love your husband have to do with our friendship? I love you both. You have always been so illogical, Yolunda.* But I understood she was responding on a purely emotional level. I wouldn't have expected anything else. So instead of saying what I believed to be the truth, I pleaded ignorance.

"Huh? What's the matter, Yolunda? I just stopped by to give Jake that herbal tea you both like so much."

It was what we planned to say if caught, so our stories wouldn't contradict each other's. A plan concocted during lovemaking and laughter, for we didn't believe we would get caught. Yolunda was more likely to work overtime than come home early. But at that moment, looking into Yolunda's eyes, the lie didn't sound right. My legs were jelly, my head humming, and your long overgrown weeds had begun talking to me, chattering wildly. Insects buzzed, as if they were as astonished as the weeds, as angry as Yolunda. I could picture the bees' furious little faces. The flies rubbing their miniscule mitts together. The noise seemed to paralyze me.

"Oh, right, Kay, do you really think I'm that stupid? Do you think I haven't noticed the way you two look at each other?"

And then, trapped in your tangled lawn, I realized she *had* been quieter lately. Somewhat curt even. I wanted to say, *Wow, Yolunda, you're so much smarter than we thought. You figured it out before Michael even, him with his fancy job and all.* I didn't want to gaslight her. She looked so pathetic in that silly uniform she had to wear to work so that you would be free to compose. Nor did I want to betray you, and the weeds were talking even faster, reaching a low roar, and then you came out and Yolunda began yelling. You looked so calm and cool in your blue jeans and bare feet, me so innocent in the white, gauzy shirt from India. Was that the day you hosed me off in the yard with the green garden snake after our first storm of love making? Whatever had happened earlier that day was blotted out by Yolunda screaming, screaming, screaming. A little like the piece you had created for your only New York commission. I must say, now, in retrospect: you were right; you were ahead of your time.

"Yo, knock off the hysterics, you're freaking Coco out," you said.

I saw her then, Coco, her fluffy little head peeking over the top of a clump of Queen Anne's Lace near your back porch. She was sitting on one of the bottom steps, her body camouflaged by the overgrown thicket. At the sight of her staring at me, everything fell silent.

I tried to call Yolunda a few times afterwards—did she tell you that? She always hung up on me the second she recognized my voice. I can't really remember the sequence of events after that, how long it was before—well, you know. How many times you and I actually spoke to one another again. The exact course of events is fuzzy now. Since it was the last thing in your life, therefore more recent to you, you would probably know better than I. (That is, if you weren't dead.)

I do know that I told Michael that Yolunda and I had had a fight over the girls. I said she was jealous that Molly was developing faster than Coco. He didn't blink an eye, took it as one of those "chick" things. In fact he accepted it so easily that I considered upping the ante, telling him Yolunda was also jealous because she thought you were making eyes at me. I wanted to know if that would get his mind going, spark some type of epiphany. Yet I have never been completely reckless. I was already worried that he would run into Yolunda. I knew she couldn't tell him anything for certain; she had no proof. All she knew was the way I had looked frozen in the weeds, my sandals' straps looped through my fingers so that the sandals dangled from my right hand. If she later went into the studio, the sounds you had going and the smells—must and sweat and semen—would support her instincts. But she could not document sounds and smells.

You and I never really saw each other after that, did we? Except that one time when you came by early in the morning, after Michael left for work. You walked right into the house, up the stairs into our room (no one locked doors back then, not in the section of Chicago where we lived), and waited for me to wake. I remember the sound of the birds outside my window. As I sat up, I pulled the sheet up with me to cover my naked breasts. You asked me to take off with you, head south. Head west. No, east. I pretended that I wanted to go, that Molly was my only obstacle. You cried. I cried. I don't know for sure what you were crying about—rejection, anger over being caught? I remember I was sobbing, *really sobbing*, for what I had lost, with you *and* with Yolunda. I think it was one of the first times I knew with certainty that all things had to end. The fact that I could have lost Michael, too, struck me for the first time when you were standing there in the bedroom I shared with him. I realized how Yolunda must have felt seeing me in her yard, a trespasser in her private world. It seemed like such a violation. (Didn't you even think about the fact that I was naked in the bed I shared with Michael?) When you begged me one last time to leave with you, I wanted to tell you that you had missed the point. The point was having *both* you and Michael. There was no point in leaving him for you. Besides, I didn't even trust your desperation, your claims of devotion. Your appearance in our bedroom occurred shortly after you had lost that big commission to Landers due to your final refusal to be co-opted—Michael heard the whole story when he stayed in the loop one night after work, went out with friends to listen to music. (By the way, Landers has made it pretty big. I see his name in credits sometimes. But I don't really hear his stuff, not the way I heard yours.) I thought maybe you were more upset about losing the commission. It is hard to lose two things at once. I told you that you had to leave. I guess it wasn't long after that that you blew your brains out on the mattress where we had made love so many times. (Where did *you* get a gun?)

Speculation was that you couldn't take being undiscovered. Probably only Yolunda—and maybe Carlos—suspected there might be something more to it. They would never tell. Carlos, given his line of work, had learned never to speak out of school. And for the sake of her sanity, Yolunda could not allow herself to believe I was that important to you. I'm still pissed at you for letting her find your body. What were you thinking? I've tried to believe you were so distraught that you didn't know what you were doing to her. I have pictured you, alone in your studio, feeling like such a screw-up, such a failure. I know how painful it is to long for a person when you realize it is too late—I know because I longed for you in that same way for weeks after you killed yourself. And then, on top of all this, your music had let you down, again. You were just enough older than the rest of us to understand that big breaks didn't always come, regardless of how much talent one possessed. And you were *so* stubborn. I'm sure Yolunda wasn't very sympathetic during that time. She did not have much of a sense of humor to begin with. I doubt my encounter with her in your back yard improved it any. Regardless of your feelings for me, I'm sure you hated to be such a disappointment to her. I try to imagine your despair, the taste of the metal barrel resting—for how long?—in the lap of your tongue, scraping the roof of your mouth. But, Jake, *really*, couldn't you come up with a better plan for having your body found?

You'll be happy to hear Yolunda never did remarry, though last I heard Coco was a little messed up. The sort of action you took has tentacles that worm far into the crevices of the future. I was in therapy for a while. But no matter how much money I paid the lady with bright white hair and yellow teeth, a different paisley scarf knotted at her throat each session (her name escapes me now, after so many years), I couldn't get her to see my problem. She thought I needed to work through my guilt, get over the fact that I played a role in your suicide. She could not conceive of the fact that I didn't feel guilty—except, maybe, a little for lying—and didn't hold myself responsible for your actions. I wanted to explore the value of what I had lost, to understand it. The guy that I took up with later, the one I *could* confess to Michael, helped me get over lying. But you. You and Me. That was something else.

I remember the sound you made chewing my hair, the dry crunch. You wanted to record it. You told me never to cut it or dye it. I promised I wouldn't. You put gobs in your mouth and chewed. It seemed like the noise was entering my skull through the individual follicles, right to my brain, rather than through my ears. I guess it was the pot. My hair fell almost to my waist back then. We thought middle-aged ladies were crazy to wear bubble cuts and do touch-ups. Wouldn't long flowing white hair be cool on a fifty-year-old, you said? Well, I can tell you, now that I'm almost there, that our bodies lose moisture with age. It isn't so easy to keep hair below one's shoulders without it becoming thin and wispy looking. And while white hair might be cool, steel gray isn't quite so striking. But who knows? Maybe I will let it grow out now. That's the only way I can avoid my colorist in the future. I don't want to use her anymore. There must be some huge hole in her life that she needs to cover by imagining her impending doom. Thinking about that hole makes me anxious. But I can't imagine confronting her or switching colorists.

When I got home from the hairdresser there was a message on the phone from Molly, a complicated plan asking me to pretend she would be visiting me this weekend in case Eric called. She was going to be with Drew in New York, his apartment, not a hotel, so there was no other number she could leave Eric. Except her cell phone, and she didn't want to have to answer Eric in front of Drew. In fact, she was calling me on her cell on the way to the airport. (Cell phones, that's a whole other story.) Her message worried me. She was taking bigger risks and implicating me. I wanted her to face her situation, understand her actions. I wanted to tell her *NO*, I would have no part of her lies, but a second later the phone rang and it was Eric asking me if Molly had arrived yet. I told him she had just gone to the store to pick up some herbal tea. He said she didn't drink tea. *No?* I asked. *I guess it's only when she's home that she likes it. A mother/daughter ritual, sipping tea and talking.*

An odd thing is that your memory is clearer to me now than it was ten—or even fifteen—years ago. As if you have been lying in wait. I don't know what happened to so many of the people we knew back then. Those who have stayed around—like Carlos and Edge (she's a grandmother now!)—have transmuted so many times that the versions of them that remain are new people. No one allows their jeans to get worn or tattered naturally anymore (they wear them dark and sleek or with holes already ripped pre-purchase by the manufacturer), and guys don't wear their hair long anymore (short and sharp as razors standing on edge). And, I suppose, in a way, everyone has "sold out"—at least by your standards. Those who didn't, well, most of them are desperate for the chance now. But it's not as bad as you might think. Even losing my looks is a bit of a relief. I still have whatever it is that attracts men but not the thing that drew even the wrong ones to me and made me do the things I regretted.

I feel myself—my whole body—sighing. It is time to get going now, get dressed, wash my face, brush my hair.

I wonder if you—wherever you are now—can hear my words on paper any better than you could hear my thoughts? I'd like to know the *timbre* of my musings, their tone; I wish you could teach me to hear them in the same way you taught me to hear the sounds of taste and touch. Is the cacophony of my written contemplation richer than words spun from my lips? Are you in an environment made of noises we never knew existed? Do you hear things you never heard before? Strange pitches and exotic notes. Heavenly sounds. Do you miss me? Listen, while I brush my hair. Can you hear it crackle?

Behind the Door

Yolunda counted out two round blue Percocet pills and handed them to the woman in the bed. Yolunda waited while the woman, whom most of the unit called "Bird Girl," propped herself up on her elbows. Then Yolunda passed her a tiny, pleated paper cup of water. Bird Girl hooked a lock of her hair behind her right ear, put one pill on her tongue, swallowed, and then did the same with the other pill.

Her real name was Alice. Freckled, with buttery blonde hair and eyes as blue as the Percocet, Alice was 25 years old but looked younger. A large bird had flown into her car window while she was on her way to pick up her wedding dress. The bird hadn't done any serious damage; the problem had occurred when Alice had pulled over and leaped from her car, neglecting in her panic to shift the car into park. She had been smacked and knocked down by the open door, her pelvic bone broken in two places. They said she had feathers in her hair when the ambulance brought her to the hospital.

Yolunda preferred patients with incisions and large wounds that she could clean and dress. If the healing was going properly, it was like magic—how the wound appeared smaller and drier each time she removed the bandage. Bird Girl didn't have any open wounds, just cuts and scratches on her face. Still, she fascinated Yolunda—the fact that she could be so badly hurt in a car accident that involved no collision, no other cars, or, most notably, no other people. And, of course, Yolunda was also drawn in by the story of the ill-fated wedding; she couldn't help but be reminded of her own tragic young marriage.

"Have a nice day," said Yolunda as she headed for the door.

"I'm supposed to be in Hawaii now. I should be on my honeymoon, but I missed my wedding and now I'm missing my honeymoon," said Alice. Her lower lip trembled. It was known on the floor that Bird Girl and her fiancée had argued about the fact that he and his brother were using the reservations for Hawaii. They had paid for the entire honeymoon package in advance, a cheap rate with the understanding that it could not be refunded or postponed, though it could be transferred to one or more people. Yolunda had been off for several days when Bird Girl arrived, so she had never seen Alice's young man.

"You'll have other chances," said Yolunda, wishing she could make her voice warmer without encouraging further conversation. Intimacy unnerved her. Then, though she didn't believe it for a second, she added, "These things usually happen for a reason."

"I'm worried that Tom will back out now. He's superstitious, thinks the bird was some kind of omen or something. When will I be able to have sex again?"

"You'll need to discuss that with your physician," said Yolunda, who, though she had a perfectly functional pelvic bone, hadn't had sex in over twenty years. If Bird Girl thought men were superstitious about women who were attacked by birds the day before their weddings, she should see how they reacted to women who were widows of suicides. Not that Yolunda had made any attempts to become involved with another man.

"Will the fractures affect my future orgasms?" Bird Girl asked plaintively.

The question made Yolunda even more uncomfortable. She was not one of the nurses patients usually confided in. And she never discussed sex, not even with her own daughter, Coco. Even with Jake, they had rarely actually *talked* about it.

"You should make a list of questions for your physician," said Yolunda, checking the chart one last time to make sure she had given all the meds. She hoped her repetition of the word "physician" made clear that she was not going to answer any questions. "Well, have a good day."

As she left the room, Yolunda made a mental note to recommend some sort of anti-depression med to the physician. She closed the door behind her, something rarely done on the floor unless a patient requested it.

* * *

Yolunda had the ability to look at a person without revealing any emotion, a useful trait both on the job and in keeping distance in her personal life. She seemed to see and not see people at the same time. Usually she wasn't conscious of how she might appear to others. But on Saturday, when she opened the door to the handsome young man, she knew how she must look—her lipless mouth, straight and grim, her eyes as unblinking as glass marbles—and didn't try to soften it. Saturday was the one day she had at home to work on her project. She had just become immersed when the doorbell rang.

"Is Coco home?" he asked, his voice polite and confident.

"Coco doesn't live here anymore," said Yolunda.

The young man waited, as if he expected more. He wore a puffy red ski jacket and khaki pants. He smiled a white toothy grin that probably got him what he wanted most of the time. Yolunda did not return the smile. She waited until she saw his face crack slightly, just a faint twitch, then she cocked her head as if to say, *anything else?*

"Well, I thought she might be home on Christmas break from college or something. Could you give me her number?"

Yolunda knew she must be intimidating. Of Slavic descent, she was tall and big boned, her limp blonde hair clipped in a practical bowl-cut.

"I can give her *your* number."

The young man blushed, and then fumbled around in his wallet for a slip of paper. Yolunda handed him a pen from the small front hall table under the mirror next to the coat rack. He quickly scribbled his name and number. Yolunda glanced at it as she closed the door and placed the paper on the table. *Mark.* The number had a north side area code. As she looked up, she caught a glimpse of herself in the mirror and remembered how embarrassed she had been by her own mother who spoke so little English. And here she was, a perfectly articulate woman with a fine command of the English language, an RN, and she spoke even less to Coco's friends than her mother had to hers. But Mark was not the type of young man who generally sought out her daughter. He was too handsome and sure of himself to be a friend of Coco's. Too proper. Too straight. Yolunda knew she would probably forget to give Coco the number. But she saw no reason for this boy's visit to change the way she interacted with her daughter. Since Jake's death, she had practiced what she thought of as an active form of noninterference. The less she interfered, the less chance she had of damaging Coco. As a result, Coco finally seemed to be developing a sense of independence and confidence. The summer before college, she had even lost some weight. Yolunda was not about to let a suave young man throw her off track.

In the end, Yolunda didn't believe her own actions mattered one way or another. If he had a legitimate reason to see Coco, he would be back.

Yolunda returned to her bedroom and her computer and promptly forgot the boy on her porch when she clicked on her site:

The Adventures of Lunda

She had started the series over ten years ago, before she purchased her first computer. The project began when her psychologist suggested she keep a journal about Jake and how she felt about what he had done. *Whatever comes into your head.* Yolunda had only gone to three more sessions because she had been embarrassed to show the psychologist her journal. Yolunda had taken enough courses in nursing school to know she was supposed to go through stages—denial, guilt, and anger—she couldn't remember the exact order anymore. But her journal had taken a different turn. A fictional one. She had written how instead of finding Jake hours after the suicide, she had gotten there just in the nick of time and wrestled the gun away. She had tried again and again to write the truth, but every time she wrote about opening the door to his studio, he was still alive, holding the gun to his temple. She had written various accounts of what happened next. In one, she dived across the room and forced the gun up so that it discharged into the ceiling, raining plaster on them. In another, she karate-kicked the weapon from his hand. In still another, she had been wounded in the struggle. The only common element was how Jake had begged her forgiveness and spent the rest of his life devoted to her. When it became apparent that the journal was never going to become what the psychologist wanted, Yolunda terminated therapy. But she couldn't stop writing the story of her saving Jake. She wrote it over and over until her head hurt from the telling, eventually taking it from paper to the computer. She was stuck in her attempts to perfect a version of how events should have transpired—*would* have if she had gotten there sooner. Sometimes she stayed up half the night, reworking, revising, getting rid of nagging details that didn't fit. She might have gone crazy if she hadn't flipped on a replay of the 10 o'clock news one insomnia-driven night to catch footage of a girl about to leap from a viaduct on the Dan Ryan Expressway. The image had sent Yolunda back to her computer and an account of her daring rescue of the girl. Adrenaline surged through Yolunda's system as she described herself edging along the shelf of the bridge, clasping the hand of the desperate girl, and guiding her to safety. From that night her character was born: Lunda! In the beginning she wrote for her own pleasure, but a few years ago she had turned her story into a blog that attracted followers.

Yolunda combined elements from the old television hero Zorro with Buffy the Vampire Slayer, a heroine Coco had liked when she was younger, and elements from her own life to create Lunda. The name choice seemed particularly fitting, since Jake had gone through a phase when he wanted her to call herself Lunda instead of Yolunda, thinking it sounded more exotic. Since she knew Zorro better from watching so many repeats of it as a child, Yolunda based most of the details on him, varying them to fit a female heroine. Instead of wearing a raccoon-ish eye mask, Lunda wore a sheer black veil that covered her nose and mouth, like a harem girl; and, instead of marking the scenes of her heroic acts with a slashed "Z," she left a large loopy 𝓛 made with a red grease pencil so that it looked like lipstick (she had tried to write about actual lipstick, but it seemed too slow and breakable); and, most important of all, instead of intervening in skirmishes between victims and villains, Lunda usually saved people from themselves.

* * *

The note on the refrigerator had said:

DON'T COME OUT TO THE STUDIO. SEND DANNY. DON'T BLAME YOURSELF. THIS HAS NOTHING TO DO WITH YOU. I'M SORRY. JAKE

The battered old refrigerator rumbled and vibrated, as if echoing the written warning, but Yolunda had not heeded it. Instead, she had grabbed four-year-old Coco from the floor where she had placed her when they had come in the door. Clutching her daughter, Yolunda had run through the weedy back yard, the long grass yellow and limp with the coming of autumn, to the studio. Yolunda's heart pounded against Coco's small chest. Her initial reaction—before she actually reached the studio—was mostly physical. Her brain felt liquid, as if it was seeping down through her arms and chest. How she hated the studio! It was the place he went to get away from them. The place he worked on his new, weird music instead of getting a real job. The place that made it necessary for her to work extra shifts—she was still a nurse's aide back then—to make up for the fact that he made so little money. The place he had gone after she quit singing with his band, continued to go after even he had quit. Worst of all, the studio was the place he had taken her supposed friend, Kay.

Nothing to do with you. A worse insult than saying it was because of her.

As she crossed the yard, she tried to convince herself that he hadn't really done anything. He had been depressed. But he had been depressed many times and not killed himself. The note was to get attention. Maybe he had swallowed a few pills, knowing Danny, his brother, would rush him to the hospital. She told herself that Jake was a narcissist. He would never really hurt himself. He just needed drama. Yet when she reached the side door to the studio, the former garage, she stopped and put Coco down.

"Go play," she said and pushed her toward the wading pool that they hadn't bothered to drain or deflate at the end of summer. A few bright plastic toys floated on the side that still held stagnant water. The other half of the pool was on a slight incline. "Play with your little boat. I need to talk to Daddy."

Even after Coco had started across the yard, Yolunda hesitated. The wooden Victorian door had been taken from a razed house two blocks away to replace the old rotten door. The replacement door had two long panels on top, one vertical panel in the center, and two more horizontal panels side by side on the bottom. The door knob was white marble, jutting from a brass lock plate etched with leafy vines. Although the paint was beginning to chip, the door was more elegant and well built than the garage-transformed-to-studio that surrounded it. Yolunda circled the white marble knob with her fingers and turned it.

* * *

The day before Alice's scheduled release, her fiancée was due back in Chicago. The floor buzzed with speculation. Someone heard his plane had landed in the early afternoon, so everyone hoped he would come directly from the airport. He could show up at anytime. Whenever the elevator door opened, the staff paused and held their breaths.

Yolunda was usually above patient gossip and conjecture, but for once she felt curious. When she saw two of the nurse assistants at the desk in deep discussion, Yolunda sauntered over and picked up a chart.

"I bet he dumps her," said Jean, a young woman with skin the color of cork board, who sat behind the desk. She had very long nails, over an inch, that curved around and inward like rigatoni. As she spoke she dabbed a sparkly polish on the tip of each nail. Yolunda was fascinated with the way Jean worked with patients, faster than most of the other assistants, though she used her hands oddly to avoid harming the nails. They curled in slightly. Almost like paws.

"If I was her, I'd kick his fat ass out," said Carmel, who leaned over the counter, watching Jean's intricate operation on her nails.

"Oh, is he fat?" asked Yolunda.

Both women turned and looked at her. Yolunda realized that it was probably the first question of that sort that she had ever asked at work. She was about to say never mind when Carmel spoke.

"Naw, that's just an expression. He's okay looking, I guess." Carmel herself, Yolunda realized, was probably forty pounds overweight.

"I think he's hot," said Jean. "I'd go out with him in a second."

Yolunda wanted to ask more but didn't want to reveal the depth of her interest, so she put down the chart and went to check on a patient whose blood pressure had been spiking earlier in the day. Later when she saw Terry, one of the more talkative orderlies, by himself at the broom and cleaning supplies closet, she approached him. He was tall and big boned, probably, like Yolunda, of Polish American descent. She didn't know his last name. His hair, like hers, was a dirty blonde, but he wore it spiky, streaked with bright yellow-white stripes.

"Hey, Terry, how you doing?" She smiled as invitingly as she could after so long without practice. "I was wondering. Could I ask you a question? Do you know what kind of bird attacked the woman in 3C?"

Happy to have an opportunity to offer his thoughts on the subject, Terry didn't even blink at the fact that Yolunda's curiosity was out of character.

"A big ole blue jay. About twice the size of a normal jay, I hear. But get this." Terry smiled, looked down, and shook his head. "She thought it might be trying to get a stick of gum she had just put in her mouth. Now, what do you think of that?"

"It sounds a little strange."

"That's what *I* think. I mean how would a bird flying overhead know about a stick of gum in a car beneath him? Jays can be mean, I know that. But how's he gonna know unless he's staked out in a tree on Ashland Ave, watching the cars go by. And could those beady little eyes really see the movement of her lips?"

"That's where it happened? On Ashland?" For some reason, Yolunda had pictured it on an expressway.

"That's where she *said* it happened. But if you ask me, the whole story is wacky. Though she couldn't be lying about everything; she had feathers in her hair."

"I heard that."

"You hear her fiancée's plane landed over two hours ago and she hasn't heard from him? He only called once from Hawaii and I hear she cried the whole time she was on the phone. They could hear it all the way down at the front desk."

Yolunda waited for more, but Terry just shook his head again, stuffed four rolls of paper towels under his right arm, cradled two more in his left, and walked away. He was still shaking his head as he turned the corner. Yolunda tried to stick it out past her shift to see the fiancée. When he hadn't come by 6:30, she couldn't find more busy work so she went home.

* * *

That night she began an episode of Lunda rescuing the Bird Girl from the crazed blue jay. It was a problem story from the start. For one thing, it was unprofessional to tell a story from work so she had to disguise or eliminate some of the best details. For another— and this was a first for Yolunda in a long time—she got stuck in the very beginning of the adventure. She couldn't figure out how to get Lunda to the scene. She kept imagining Lunda swooping down from above. But from the start of the series, she had avoided imbuing Lunda with supernatural powers. Where was the heroism if Lunda could do things magically? And there was no way Lunda could reach from the driver's side of her own car into Bird Girl's. Finally, Yolunda settled on Lunda riding up on a motorcycle. Yolunda hoped this new detail wouldn't be too much of a jolt to her readers, given Lunda had never before driven a motorcycle. When Yolunda had begun the series, consistency and realism hadn't been a first priority—but now that she was online, with over 100 hits for every new episode, she had to think about Lunda's fans. (Yolunda did know how a motorcycle felt since Jake's brother, Danny, had owned one, which she had ridden on twice back when she still sang with Jake's band.) Yolunda cherished the complimentary e-mails she got from readers but grew disproportionately depressed when a fan criticized her, pointing out an inconsistency or unbelievable detail. But almost as soon as she added the motorcycle, she was stuck again. When she reached the part where Lunda reaches in and snatches the bird from the window—"a flurry of blue feathers, talons, and squawks"—she couldn't get Lunda off the bike and into the car fast enough to shove the gear into park. It seemed cheating to not deal with that part at all, except if there was no longer a bird, why would Bird Girl even leap out of the car? Frustrated, Yolunda finally went to bed. She had a six-to-six shift the following day and it was nearly midnight.

She couldn't sleep. Her mind raced and the bed seemed too warm. The pillow felt hot against her cheek. Yolunda kicked off the covers and padded to the dining room where she lowered the temperature from 68 to 66. She didn't want to wake up freezing in a few hours. Still, she couldn't sleep. She thought of Alice, the distress in her voice. Yolunda closed her eyes and counted backwards. She didn't fall asleep immediately, yet images of Bird Girl, the tiny circles of blue Percocet on her pink tongue, then Jake, his hand on the strings of his old guitar, the fanning of his finger bones like the spread claws of a bird, skipped across her consciousness.

* * *

As she had twisted the white marble knob, Yolunda had known. Maybe it was from the perfect quiet on the other side of the studio door. Or maybe it was a more spiritual sort of knowledge. The way she had been poised, waiting for something final to happen.

Yolunda had been a nurse's aide when they met. Jake had been a student at University of Illinois—"Circle," they called it back then. A friend, another nurse's aide, saw the flier and convinced Yolunda to try out as a singer in Jake's band. She remembered how he had sat, the first time he listened to her, legs straddled on either side of a ladder-back chair turned backwards. He had said he loved the purity of her voice, the clarity. One perfect year. Her hair a river of blonde flowing between her shoulder blades. Her size suddenly powerful and sexy, rather than large and gawky. The big hoop earrings he bought her. The way he looked at her. Her voice clear and cool. Their wedding in the basement of city hall. The band and Jake's friends crowded into the judge's chambers. Daisies in her hair. The smell of the freshly mimeographed sheets of paper they were given to read. Afterwards, going to Old Town for pizza. Another year, almost as good. Coco's birth. Jake assisting in the delivery, a tape of their band in the background. Jake recording it all so that Coco's first cries mingled with their music. Taking Coco to gigs at first. Later being forced out of the band to make more money. The next year, it all fell apart. Working all day, waiting up late for Jake at night. Later and later. Sometimes not at all. His growing disdain for the kind of music the band made, *they* had made, as he moved into "audio art," just a bunch of sounds she couldn't understand. Jake quitting the band and going to grad school. Inheriting his grandmother's house. The three of them moving in without the joy a young family should feel in their first house. Transforming the garage into a studio. His talking less, staying out more, even without a band. It was as if she had been sucked into a whirling tornado, been at the center for a while, then spit out at the same place where she had been scooped up, only now with a baby in her arms.

Yolunda turned the knob until it would go no further.

* * *

Alice already sat propped up against her pillows when Yolunda entered to give her meds. She had made up her young face as perfectly as a covergirl. Because of the mascara and shadow, her blue eyes looked rounder and bigger, almost twice their natural size, though also a little red-rimmed. None of the scratches showed on her face. In fact her skin looked almost artificial in its flawlessness.

"He hasn't even come to see me yet."

"Your fiancée?" Yolunda asked, puzzled. She had assumed she had missed all the drama the night before.

Alice was about to respond when the fiancée strode into the room, tan, handsome, and confident. Yolunda was surprised by the sudden jolt of hatred she felt. A feeling almost as intense as what she had felt for Jake's studio. The fiancée carried a little package wrapped in blue tissue paper as confidently as he held Bird Girl's future in his hands. At least the package offered hope.

"I'll come back when your company leaves," said Yolunda and left the room, closing the door behind her. A small crowd awaited her at the desk. Carmel was the first to speak.

"Well, what happened? What did he say?"

"I don't know," Yolunda said. "I left before either of them said anything."

A collective sigh issued from the group.

Nervously tapping her long, serpentine nails, Jean spoke next.

"You could have at least left the door open."

The remark was slightly impertinent, yet it gave Yolunda a sense of inclusion. Before she had asked about Bird Girl, an assistant would not have spoken to her in such a familiar way. They waited, offering varying opinions, for what seemed like ten minutes. But when no shouts or sobs came from behind the door in that time, Yolunda decided they should return to work. She wasn't the head nurse, but she was the senior nurse on duty and should assume some responsibility.

"We should all go about our business." When no one moved, she clapped her hands. The gesture, she knew, was fussy but effective.

Grumbling, the group slowly dispersed. Yet no one, including Yolunda, strayed far from the front desk or room 3C unless absolutely necessary. Forty-five minutes passed with tortured slowness. When Yolunda passed Carmel and Jean, Carmel asked, "What the hell could be taking so long?"

"It's a bad sign, isn't it? He must be ending it," said Jean. "You think that package was a sorry little goodbye gift?"

"Maybe it was a package of rubbers and they're in there screwing right now," said Carmel. "It's happened here before."

All three of them laughed.

Another twenty minutes passed. Yolunda and Jean went into 3F to change a dressing and to sponge bathe a patient. Yolunda watched Jean's bright nails flash in the sunlight from the window as she unrolled bandages.

"You know, when we're finished here, I am going to have to go back in 3C no matter what," said Yolunda, as if thinking aloud. "I only gave Bird Girl one of her meds. If I don't finish soon, she'll be off cycle."

"You go, girl. She need her meds," said Jean. "We best snap this up then."

A week ago, Yolunda would have never made such a confession to a colleague. Particularly a subordinate. Of course a week ago, she realized, she never would have left the room before completing the meds. She never would have expected a girl who was brought in with a crown of blue feathers in her hair to have had such an effect on her.

Almost simultaneous with their exit from 3F, the door to 3C opened. The fiancée walked out quickly, a determined frown on his face. He stared straight ahead and didn't look at anyone as he waited for the elevator, stabbing the "down" button three or four times in rapid succession.

"Anxious to leave the scene of the crime," mumbled Jean, hands in knots on her hips, nails curled inward. "Make a clean get-away."

They watched as he disappeared through the slit of the automatic door.

"Well, wish me luck," said Yolunda as she went to the desk to retrieve her chart and med tray. She took a deep breath before pushing down the chrome handle to Bird Girl's room.

Bird Girl sat propped up in the same position as when Yolunda had last seen her. Except for a slight smudge of mascara under her right eye, her make-up appeared undisturbed. The box, still tied with the ribbon, was on the middle of the floor between the bed and the door. Balancing the med tray and chart in one hand, Yolunda stooped to retrieve the box.

"Thanks," said Bird Girl.

"Are you all right, Alice?" asked Yolunda. She had not spoken Bird Girl's name aloud before. She thought of her alternately as Bird Girl and Alice.

"Fine. Good, I think," said Alice, nodding her head as if to confirm it. "I'm good. I broke up with him."

"*What?*" asked Yolunda, placing the box on the bedside table.

"I thought about what you told me and I stuck to it," said Alice.

"I told you? What? What did I tell you?" Yolunda could not remember offering any advice. She felt a swell of panic in her throat, a sensation she had not experienced in many years. Dizzy, lightness in her head. She had been careful for so long not to interfere in anyone's life. She did not want to be held responsible for anyone's pain. What could she have possibly said to induce this young woman to make such a major decision?

"You know, how 'everything happens for a reason.' I've thought about that a lot over the last few days. Kevin called it an omen, but maybe it was a *good* omen. An experience that was supposed to make me stop and think."

Yolunda wanted to shout, *but that was a throw-away line, a cliché*, yet she was too stunned to speak.

"I moved out here to Illinois for *him*. I hardly have any friends here, none of my family. Then when I get hurt, what does he do? He worries about *himself*, what it might mean to him, if he was going to lose money on our honeymoon! If you hadn't said what you said, I probably would have gone back with him. I've felt so miserable and scared. More needy than I've ever been. But I kept asking myself *what was the reason?* And I decided it was so I could learn how self-centered Kevin is before I married him."

"You mean he still wanted to get married?"

"He said he had 'meditated' on it while he was lying on the beach in Hawaii, had discussed it for hours with his brother, and had decided he was willing to keep his commitment. Can you imagine? *Willing?*"

"What's in the box?"

"I don't know," said Alice. "I didn't open it. I didn't want to change my mind."

* * *

Yolunda was excited on the ride home. She knew exactly how she would finish the Bird Girl episode. For the first time, one of her subjects was going to play a greater role in saving herself than Lunda. Yolunda dropped her coat on the living room couch as she rushed to the computer. She clicked open the site, but a peculiar thing happened as she began typing. She found she wasn't writing the remainder of the Lunda episode. She was writing about that afternoon, many years ago, picking up where she had left off, her hand on the doorknob to Jake's studio.

Yet this time when the knob stopped turning, Yolunda wrote about what really happened after she pushed inward. How the smell hit her—must mingled with blood. A butcher store. She thought of hamburger left on the counter too long to defrost. The thought that a human's blood, her husband's, could smell like an animal's startled her. Then she felt guilty to think such a thing. Then guilty to think anything rational at all. To not simply *feel*. She saw Jake on the old mattress, his bare feet sticking up from the end facing her, his head out of sight, at the far end where the mattress sloped down slightly. The sight of his bare feet gave her a second of hope—he wouldn't kill himself without being fully dressed, would he?—but the thought barely surfaced before it was dashed. There was no etiquette for suicide. No proper dress. (Later she would learn differently when people fussed about how there hadn't been more of a note than what was left on the refrigerator, and then she learned of Jake's thoughtfulness when the sheriff's office told her Jake had first covered the mattress with oil cloth to protect it from blood.) Yolunda moved forward a step, to see his head, to make sure. She looked quickly, only once. His right eye was open, unblinking, staring at the ceiling; the left half of his face was a brownish red, except for the socket where the blood had pooled and, therefore, failed to congeal, making it brighter. A congealing red sea. She didn't remember screaming or even gasping, just observing, quickly. His t-shirt seemed saturated, but her eyes didn't rest long enough to be sure. On the table, by his feet, was his whirring recorder and an envelope with Danny's name written across the front. Yolunda grabbed the envelope and turned to leave, then stopped, suddenly, and touched Jake's toes, just brushed the fingers of her left hand across them. They were paler in death, but still lovely. The sweep of his metatarsal bones looked elegant. Jake had had beautiful hands and feet.

Yolunda wrote all of this, and wrote how she had closed the door behind her before running across the yard to scoop up Coco. She wrote about calling the police. She wrote about polishing the dining room table with lemon Pledge as she waited—a detail she had completely forgotten until she typed it. She wrote about the police taking the gun and the recorder, about people arriving and about how she hadn't even remembered stuffing the envelope with Danny's name in the bottom of her underwear drawer until she came across it days later. She had considered giving it to Danny, but had put it off for so long that the opportunity had passed. She never opened the envelope. She wrote that she still wasn't sure if that was because she was frightened of the contents or because she was embarrassed that Jake had taken the time to write his brother a sealed letter but had only scribbled a refrigerator note for her. He had cared more about preserving the surface of the old mattress than providing her with an explanation.

When she finished writing, Yolunda was exhausted. Her very bones felt weary. Though it was hours before she usually went to bed, she fell asleep almost as soon as she pulled up the covers. The next morning, she slept in a little later than usual, luxuriating in the feel of her sheets, the softness of her pillow. She knew she would be late for work, but she took a moment to remove the envelope that had resided all these years at the bottom of her drawer, visible only when she was behind with laundry. She scribbled an apology and her first initial in the place for the return address, wrote Danny's address under his name, and stuck two stamps in the corner. She was half way down her front steps when, as an afterthought, she went back up and inside and found the slip of paper with the number of the boy who had stopped by to see Coco. She looked at it again. The number and the name. Mark. She was already fifteen minutes late, the latest she had ever been for her shift. She placed the paper back on the table. There would be time later to call Coco with the boy's number. For now, she needed to drive to the post office and stick the envelope in the slot before she had a chance to reconsider.

Second Sight

The worst part was the embarrassment. People looked at me with sympathy, with *sadness*, thinking that was what I felt. And I *was* sad, but never—at least until I reached my twenties—was it the overriding emotion. It was red, burning shame, as tangible as a thing.

Like the suicide. Not an act, but a thing. The-suicide-of-my-father.

When I was little, just the absence was embarrassing. Not having a father was like not having a bike, the right brand of shoes, permission to go on a fieldtrip. Even the kids whose parents were divorced had fathers *somewhere*, fathers who came on weekends or took their children on expensive trips. For me, "father" signified an empty hole. A hole that widened and deepened when, around the age of eight, I learned what suicide meant. Before then, the word had just been another mysterious grown-up word, like operation, laxative, or pesticide. I loosely connected the word with death, the same way I connected "operation" with going to the hospital. When I was told the real meaning, I actually lost my vision for a moment, heard the echo of the hollow hole. My father had intentionally left, removed himself permanently from the world and the possibility of seeing me again. *By choice.* He had blown his brains out in order to get away as fast as he could. It was so embarrassing! Like a loud fart in a crowded room that no one ever mentions. Everyone merrily pretending the rudeness never occurred. The-suicide-of-my-father. The ultimate breach of etiquette.

No wonder I was so drawn to Roy, an older man who trafficked in death and the many twisted and varied roads to it.

* * *

I learned what suicide meant when I was eight years old and Dennis, a boy at Edge's Day Care, told me. I loved the daycare, a makeshift place at the home of a friend of my mother's named Edge, a woman with five children of her own. Edge had transformed the backyard on her long, narrow city lot into a magical playground at very little expense. There was a huge sandbox that she had filled (and kept full) by having each child carry two plastic buckets of sand back from Lake Michigan whenever they went to the beach; a multi-chute slide constructed from used car parts she had found at the junk yard, including a well-waxed fender she had pounded out; and, finally, a wading pool slightly larger than the sandbox. She had mixed and poured the cement to decorate the pool's rim with smooth sides of colorful broken pottery she had saved.

The kids who attended the daycare after school on week days were called dragonflies. The little kids who stayed most of the day were bumblebees. The kids who only came occasionally were designated butterflies. And the teenagers who helped out from time to time were called unicorns. Dennis and I were both dragonflies. He had only been going to Edge's for about a year. I had been going as far back as I could remember. The weather was still warm the day he told me, so we were outside on the playground. Dennis and I sat across the sandbox from each other, both longing to play but feeling too old to join the bumblebees. He was chubby with rubbery lips and was, as far as I can remember, the only child there that I disliked.

"Cuckoo," he said, "Cuckoo clock, what time is it? Or are you too fat to tell time?"

Why wouldn't a fat person be able to tell time? Besides, I wasn't fat—not yet.

"My name is Coco and I'm not fat."

"Are too fat."

Dennis was wearing a Batman t-shirt that stretched across his belly in a way that made the yellow wings elongate and fold. I sensed that he was baiting me, hoping I would react so that he would have cause—for what, I didn't know.

"Am not."

"You're so fat that your dad shot himself with a gun in the head and his brains splattered all over the place."

My confusion was replaced with a sudden burst of righteous anger. Yet I also felt unsteady, as if Dennis had the advantage. I sensed he wasn't finished—he knew more than I did. I told myself to walk away, but I couldn't. I wanted to know what he knew.

"No way. He died of suicide." I didn't like the way my voice sounded uncertain and my heartbeat seemed to quicken. What was wrong? I knew what I said was a fact.

Dennis laughed. I'll never forget it, his derision was so great that a piece of snot shot from his nose.

"What do you think suicide is, Cuckoo clock? It's killing yourself because you hate your life."

That's when I lost awareness and control of my body and fell backwards into the hole that was my father. I woke up on the ground next to the sandbox; it must have been no more than seconds later since the kids in the sandbox were in the same position. Only Dennis was gone.

When I told my mother what Dennis had said, she gasped, which was a big show of emotion for my mother. She questioned me about Dennis and daycare in general, asking me how much I liked it and whether the unicorns still helped me with my homework. I waited until she was finished to ask the crucial question.

"Is what Dennis said true?"

"Technically," she said, but her eyes darted away. I could tell her mind was already elsewhere. "But it's best not to talk about it now. Maybe when you're older."

I never went back to Edge's Day Care after that. I became a latchkey. I was instructed to wait in the house the two hours after school until my mother got home from work. I was told to call my mother the minute I walked inside, then read or do homework. I was not allowed to watch television or go outside. If someone called for my mother, I had three stories I was to rotate: she had company, she was in the basement doing laundry, or she was out in the yard, shoveling, raking, or mowing, depending on the season. The odd thing was that I never disobeyed. In truth, I actually overcompensated. I would pull one of the dining room chairs into the front hall so that it faced the front door—book and notepad in my lap—and wait, reading and eating, glancing at the front door every few minutes, nervous that my mother might not come home at all that day.

I thought of the chair as a little island, the pile of boots and umbrellas under the hat tree in the corner as a distant shore. The hardwood between the two was water that would evaporate if the phone rang or my mother walked in. Otherwise I didn't even leave to go to the bathroom. I came to know that hallway so well—every minute ripple in the wallpaper, chip in the baseboard—that I'm sure if I were transported back to it today, it would seem as if I had never left.

I kept a supply of food and snacks on the floor beneath the chair. That was when I *did* start to get fat. In the quietness of the little Chicago bungalow, with most of the neighbors still at work, my hoard of food—Saltine crackers, Twinkies, baked goods from my grandmother, and whatever odds and ends I could find in the fridge, leftovers, baloney, or Maraschino cherries—was my only comfort.

A few times, in the beginning, my mother said I didn't need to wait by the front door. She suggested I go in my bedroom or sit at the dining room table. But *only* a few times, and rather feebly. I think she liked to know exactly where she would find me when she returned home.

* * *

I had what my mom called "regular" friends until I was eleven. Play dates sometimes on Saturdays. Girls who wore brand name clothing and collected stickers. Girls who had crushes on boys, shared favorite TV shows, and wanted to be doctors or lawyers (modeling or acting in their spare time) when they grew up. But with each few pounds I gained, another friend seemed to drift away. In seventh grade, in order to fill my growing free time, I took up the clarinet. I thought I might go into music like my dad. Or I suppose I was trying—on a level I didn't understand at the time—to find out who he was, what moved him.

I loved my clarinet, the authority I felt when I screwed together the black pieces. I took great care of it, cleaning the pipes each night with a special rounded brush, then polishing the silver keys. I loved that I owned such a valuable and important item. Most of all, I loved watching my fingers work the holes, hearing the individual sounds merge to make one fluid blend. When I put the instrument into its red velvet case at night—each part in its own red-lined, fitted compartment—I felt as if I were putting a beloved child to bed. Mom got me private lessons and I joined the school band. I learned quickly. It didn't take me long to advance to first clarinet.

So, for a while, I had "band" friends, mostly nerds but also a few popular kids who wanted to play instruments. In the context of the band setting, they seemed to forget my own unpopularity. I even had a crush on one, Mark Pulaski, who played the drums and had white-blonde hair that jutted out over his brow like a little platinum cliff. The band might have remained the perfect activity for me if I hadn't continued to gain weight through seventh and eighth grade, making the prospect of the high school marching band terrifying. I knew they herded everyone into the small gym when they did fittings. I imagined Mark and the others listening as Mrs. Hautman called out the inches of my bust, waist, hips, and thighs to the student selected to record them in the book. The boys would be on the other side of a partition, but I learned from stories of kids who had older brothers and sisters in the band that they could hear. Almost as frightening was the thought of marching across the field in front of the crowded bleachers in the scratchy wool uniform, balancing the stovepipe hat on my head, trying to play and march at the same time—I have always been uncoordinated. Worst of all was the possibility of someone shouting out, "Hey, thunder-thighs, Doyle!"

I begged to be sent to a private school or move to one of the suburbs. But Mom said we didn't have the money for either. The suicide had nullified my father's insurance. My father had inherited the bungalow, which—even in our modest neighborhood—was considered in need of repair. We could never sell it for enough to live in the burbs. It was all his parents had owned. My mother's mother cleaned houses for a living. And what little money my mother had saved was for my college education.

At the end of eighth grade, I was 5'4" and 168 pounds. ("Such a pretty face," Grandma, my mom's mother, would say. "Such a shame.") I wore my thin, straight hair long and began to experiment with eye make-up. I took solace in the fact that I *did* have a pretty face, especially if I tucked my hand under my chin in a way that got rid of the roll of fat starting to double beneath it. I practiced for long periods of time in front of the bathroom mirror. The-pretty-faced-fat-girl, demure with her chin resting on her curved knuckles. I would look hideous in the band uniform with the double-breasted jacket and the big pleated pants.

After the final eighth-grade performance—where I played more elegantly and beautifully than ever before—I had a revelation. Still in the afterglow, I undressed to clean my clarinet. Clothes constrained me too much to do a proper job. I sat in my slip, cross-legged on my bed, and placed the instrument so that it traversed my knees. As usual, I was very careful, removing the reed and placing it in the glass on my bedside table before untwisting the parts. I liked how loosening a part felt like I had opened a tightly sealed bottle of Maraschino cherries. The entire process was pleasurable. Then something happened that never had before. When I removed the bell from the central pipe, a long trail of spit gushed out onto my plump knee. The sight sickened me. I gagged. There was always saliva in the pipes when I cleaned, but never so much and never before had it spilled onto my flesh. As I wiped the slime from my leg, I became convinced that was all my music amounted to—a river of spit. I quit the band the next day, thereby avoiding the ordeal of the fitting and the heavy uniform. Mom didn't object; she had created her own insular world from which she emerged only in a half-hearted way. She would comment on my actions but never make much of an effort to persuade me one way or the other. I never regretted my decision.

* * *

I can't say I hated high school. A person like me should have, but I didn't, thanks to hooking up with what some people called "the hoods." (I heard my mother telling Grandma that I "ran with the wrong crowd," which made me think of a pack of gazelles running through the plains of Africa, an image that elevated all of us.) The hoods weren't as judgmental as the other kids. And as part of that group, I could detract from my weight and lame hair with lots of make-up and jewelry and no one cared. If you had sex with a guy or gave him a blow job, he treated you the same the next day. It was understood that it was just an act you were able to perform for him better than he could for himself, the same way he was better at lifting heavy objects for you. Afterwards, if he said he would call, he did. Not like Mark Pulaski from the band.

In tenth grade, Mark had the same final period Geometry class as me. Except for passing in the hall—where he refused to make eye contact—we had rarely seen each other since band. One fine October afternoon, he caught up with me after class.

"You still play the clarinet?" he asked.

"I take it out of the case now and then, but not really," I was a little uncomfortable walking next to him, conscious of the way my hips lumbered along. I had passed the 170 pound mark by then.

"You live on Wolcott, don't you? I'll walk you home."

No one had ever walked me home before. We were quiet as we walked. It was the perfect time of afternoon, sun filtered through the autumn leaves, creating a red and yellow canopy of stained glass. The air was thick with the sweet smell of dying flowers. In my mother's living room he kissed me. I pulled him to the floor. I didn't want his hands on my hips. I wanted my body flat beneath him. We had sex between the sofa and coffee table, my skirt pulled up to my waist. His dick was slick and skinny like a wet pencil. It was over quickly. He stood up and zipped his pants.

"May I have a glass of water?" he asked.

"In the kitchen," I said. I didn't want him to witness me hoisting myself back up by pulling on the arm of the couch.

Like most Chicago bungalows, ours was railroad style, the living room in the front, next the dining room, and then the kitchen. By the time I got to the kitchen, he had finished the water and was rinsing his glass in the sink.

"I'll call you," he said and left by the back door, not able, I assumed, to face the scene of the crime. I knew he wouldn't call and he didn't. I saved the glass he had drunk from in my bedroom as a souvenir. A month or so later, Benny, a high school drop-out who still hung around the school, and I were out driving late at night, passing the lonely hours until morning together. When we stopped at an intersection next to a low building of office suites, I had an inspiration. Dozens of thick Chicago phone books were bound and stacked in the brightly-lit glass lobby. Amazingly the lobby was unlocked. We quickly piled the phone books into Benny's car trunk. A couple of blocks from the building, we pulled into a parking lot where Benny slit the strings binding the books and I circled my phone number in each of them, then we drove over to Belle Plaine. Mark's parents owned a two-flat there. I told Benny that Mark was someone I needed to prank. He didn't ask why. We opened all of the books—there must have been over forty—face up to my page on his front lawn, with my mom's number circled. The entire yard was covered. It rained before morning, poured, so that his family must have woken to a lawn of sodden phone books. I wondered if the wind and rain had destroyed my circled numbers—or, if not, whether Mark had even noticed it was my number, whether he remembered my last name.

No, I didn't hate high school. Despite incidents like the one with Mark, I managed to have some fun. There were nights of drugs and sex and laughter. Nights where all the lines blurred. I loved applying my make-up to go out, circling my eyes in dark liner, coloring the lids shades of gold and brown. I liked putting on my big hoop earrings and bangles that went all the way up to my elbows. I liked the nights of ecstasy parties in warehouses on the west side, where I would cover my upper lip and chest with Vicks VapoRub before I swallowed anything so that when I was high I could just recline on an old sofa and become my breath, my lungs, the usually natural function intensified and sharpened by the drug and the Vicks. Feather boy would skate past on his roller blades and dust me with his feather duster. Whatever part of me he swiped—my face, my leg, my hand—felt as if a dozen butterflies were fluttering their fragile wings against my skin. There were boys like Benny to make out with and screw. And there were nights when I forgot that I had ever even had a father. But when I am honest, I know those nights were in the minority, and weren't even as much fun as I pretended.

Certainly there were more nights when I considered ending it. Nights when I imagined running a blade along the upper inside of each thigh where they connected with the pelvic region, the pleasure of clearly delineating where my legs met my nether regions, inside the folds of fat. Of watching the blood trickle out. Of running a new blade down the inside of my forearms, splitting them open like the white underbellies of fish. These were dreamy times when I thought it would be peaceful to combine the-pretty-faced fat-girl and the-suicide-of-my-father. Slip into a warm bath with all my connecting places slit. Nights when I thought I could find true solace that way, when I had to draw on all my strength to keep from following my father.

* * *

Things changed when Benny took me to a dealer's house, an older guy who turned out to have known my dad. There were a couple of guys smoking pot on the sofa. I had been in similar scenes a million times, guys-on-a-couch-getting-high. At Carlos's, the scene was slightly more upscale. The couch and the chairs at either end were buttery brown leather and the glass coffee table had fancy wrought iron legs, but the debris strewn across the table surface—half-full beer bottles, empty Mountain Dew cans, and overflowing ashtrays—was the same. And so were the slant-eyed-high looks of the guys on the couch. They were just older, hippie types rather than the dudes my own age I was used to.

Benny sat on the couch between the two guys, testing the pot. They were both big guys, which made him look smaller and younger. Benny was skinny with faint acne and a wispy, translucent mustache. Carlos, the dealer, sat in the chair at the far end. I tentatively resided on the arm of the other chair.

"Pretty good stuff," Benny said between tokes.

"*Pretty* good? That shit is Baja! Four star. The best," said Carlos. "I deal only in pot, which allows me to concentrate on quality. You usually buy from the Turk, don't you? I don't know how he stays in business. The shit he peddles is embarrassing."

The entire time he talked, Carlos leaned forward a little too solicitously, making me think of a particularly ardent talk show host—or maybe it was simply the arrangement of the couch and chairs, the talk show configuration. He had thinning black hair, worn in a skimpy little pony tail, the kind older, balding men favored for a while—like a cotton puff bound with a rubber band—deluding themselves that others might think a ponytail meant they had lush hair. Carlos seemed smarmy.

"What's your girlfriend's name?" he asked, referring to me.

I stiffened and waited, grateful for the fact that Benny hadn't protested the assumption too loudly or quickly.

"We're just friends," Benny said.

"Coco's my name," I said.

"Cool name," said the bigger of the two huge guys on the couch. Though not much younger than Carlos, he had still-thick bushy brown hair worn to his shoulders. A thick brown beard. He wore a tent-like, yellow Hawaiian shirt covered with hula girls and palm trees.

Carlos rolled my name around on his tongue. "Coco. Coco. I knew a guy once with a kid named Coco, a musician who named her after some blues singer. You couldn't . . . no, man, you're way too old. What's your last name?"

"Doyle."

Carlos slapped his forehead.

"Shit, no, Jake Doyle's kid. Jesus. I knew that guy. Half Mick, half Polack. He was a great musician, composed some far-out stuff. Shit. He waxed himself. Blew his brains out in his own backyard studio."

The echo reverberated in my head. My vision blurred. Our garage? The garage that had been converted to a room that we had never—as far as I knew—used. In my mind's eye, I saw the rusted padlock on the door. No one had told me. My reaction must have registered on my face because Carlos responded.

"Shit, man, I'm an insensitive bastard."

"It's okay," I said. "I know how he went out." My tone, I hoped, was appropriately hard. It must have been because Carlos returned to his reverie.

"Shit. Jake Doyle. I haven't thought of him in years. Wow, second generation of doing business. This is a first—that I know of. I'm giving you a nickel bag on the house."

Benny glanced at me, a new look of admiration on his face. For me, it was another revelation. Just as my mother never told me where my father had killed himself, she never told me he did drugs. But it all made a kind of sense. After all, he was a musician. Wouldn't he smoke pot? And the garage going unused had always seemed odd. As misanthropic as my mother could be, she was a pragmatic person. We could have stored things in it or easily have converted it back into a garage. It would have saved her years of shoveling snow from her windshield. During my junior year I had pleaded with her to allow me to make it into a bedroom for myself but she—usually not one to argue if I did the work—refused to even consider it.

"You ever try to contact him?"

The question startled me. It was the big, hairy guy talking, the one in the Hawaiian shirt.

"Huh? Who?" I wasn't even certain the question was aimed at me.

"Roy's a psychic," said Carlos.

"Look me up. I can help you contact your old man. I'm on North Lincoln," he said, pulling a white business card from the breast pocket of his shirt, sticking his arm out to indicate that I was expected to lean forward and take it. I glanced at it quickly before dropping it in my purse. In black lettering it read:

The Other Realm
Readings by Roy Reeves

Next to the lettering was a tiny crystal ball.

After we left, Benny took me to Baker's Square where we ate a whole chocolate silk pie. Where did he put it? Before he took me home, we drove out behind a warehouse on Clyburn. We moved to the back seat and I gave him a blow job. I sensed more enthusiasm in his pelvic thrusts than usual, yet also more restraint and consideration. Rather than yank my hair as he moved, he petted it gently.

* * *

Roy's "Other Realm" was located in an old frame storefront, leaning so far to the left that it looked like one strong kick could send it reeling. The building was narrow in the front but extended a long way in the back. Roy, in a red Hawaiian shirt adorned with swinging monkeys, stood behind the counter. Standing, he was even more massive than he had appeared on the couch, probably 6'3" and over 300 pounds. With his bushy hair and beard and pink face, he resembled one of those big-time wrestlers you see on television. Yet under his heavy brow, his piercing blue eyes reflected intelligence, kindness, humor and something else—sadness, maybe. A strange mixture, particularly for someone who didn't look very smart at first glance. I couldn't guess his age—forty? Forty-five? I wasn't much good at deciphering the age of anyone over thirty.

"Well, well, if it ain't little Coco Bean," he said. "I've been expecting you." A shiver spread through my chest. It had been weeks since I met him at Carlos's house.

He showed me around his shop, plywood shelves crowded with incense, magic oils, crystals, and yellowing books on astral flight, astrology, magic and witchcraft, most covered with a thin layer of dust. Absent-mindedly I ran my finger along the edge of one shelf, watching it collect gummy dirt. He seemed to read my thoughts.

"Most of my business is in readings. I don't sell much," he said. "So, you ready to go for it?"

Through a beaded curtain, we entered a series of cramped little rooms and back hallways. The floors were slightly slanted— though not as much as they appeared from the outside—and the walls were papered in brittle, old newspaper clippings. Hundreds of articles, yet I had the feeling they all held meaning for Roy. It wasn't just random papering. The passageway twisted and turned. As we got deeper inside, I grew frightened—a feeling I had rarely experienced since the days I spent waiting for my mother in the front hallway. The middle of the building opened into a room that hosted a doctor's examination table, padded black vinyl—covered with a dirty, nubby white towel—on a broad steel pedestal base. Again, Roy read my mind. As we passed through to the continuing hallway, he said, "I do healing oil massages there. I'm trained as a masseur."

The building ended in a small sun room walled in windows, each with multiple panes painted black, though sunlight leaked along the seams and in a few chipped places. Roy cleared off a space on a rickety table piled with newspapers. He placed a crystal ball on the table and a deck of Tarot cards with edges so grimy that I had to look away to avoid feeling queasy. He stood perfectly quiet for a moment with his eyes closed.

"I think we'll do the cards today," he said, opening his eyes at the same time. Then he pulled up a chair for each of us.

When he shuffled the cards, I saw the lines of dirt beneath his nails. I watched the arch of cards blur between his hands. Afterward he expertly slapped down a pattern of individual cards. I noticed what seemed to be a preponderance of Death cards.

"Don't worry, Death doesn't always mean death."

I wish I had written down everything he said that day because I remember so little. I slipped in and out of association, tumbling in and out of the void that was my father. The one thing Roy said that clearly stood out was that my father was with me. He hadn't been for a while, but he was back watching over me. Roy also said that my life would improve. The Death cards signaled the end of a difficult period in my life. As he slid the cards back into a pile, he told me the reading was $50, but I didn't have to pay if I thought we were going to be seeing more of each other. I said yes, I did, and he took me by the hand back to the room with the massage table.

He undressed me, slowly, carefully slipping the individual disks of my buttons through their separate slits. I had had sex with at least six guys and given blow jobs to even more, but no one had ever seen me naked. I thought of the Madonna song, "Like a Virgin," and laughed.

"What?" he asked, looking up at me with his cloudless blue eyes from where he knelt before me unbuttoning.

"Nothing," I said.

Because of his size, I didn't feel fat or embarrassed as I stood before him naked. He looked up at me from his knees, then stood and slipped out of his own clothing. He was huge and white. Except for the fact that his body, from the neck down, was relatively hairless, he reminded me of one of the great apes at the Lincoln Park Zoo. When he was completely naked, he hoisted himself onto the table and guided me up on top of him. I had never been on top before. In truth, I didn't even know that the woman *could* be on top. He shifted me onto his penis, the head swollen to the size of a large plum, clamped one huge hand on my butt, the other on my back, and began moving me around in circular motions, almost as if he were rubbing himself and I were part of his belly. At first I was confused; I was used to the guy moving while I lay perfectly still. Then I began to understand the rhythm, the concept, and began to assist in moving myself in sweeping circles. Around and around. A strange and wonderful loosening opened in my groin; I moved faster to abet it. Around and around, moistening, opening, around and around, faster.

"Come on, Coco Bean," he whispered.

It was wonderful, like swimming or flying, only instead of using water or air as a medium, I was using his body. I put my arms out to my sides like wings. I was soaring. He freed his right hand from my back to squeeze my right nipple, while his left hand rotated my butt even faster. His face was flushed a deep crimson.

"Okay, Coco Bean, bring it home, baby, bring it home."

Something incredible inside me burst, like an exotic flower suddenly erupting into bloom, continuing to unfurl and open, becoming fuller and fuller than I thought possible until, at the moment of what I realized was climax, I saw the face of my father and I screamed.

* * *

Two days after graduation, I hocked my clarinet and stereo, and moved in with Roy. Mom didn't mind—I told her that I was living with a bunch of people, just friends, guys and girls, in a group house. As long as I stopped home once or twice a week, she didn't inquire further or ask to visit me. ("I can imagine it," she told Grandma. "Why depress myself further by actually seeing the place in reality?")

The first week, I spent most of my time in his little apartment over the shop—there were plenty of rooms up there, but they were all crowded with boxes, books, broken furniture and other junk. You couldn't even open the door to some of them. In the space where he lived was a little stove and a fridge, a bed, two dressers, and a television. The television didn't have much reception. That first week I watched soaps. All I could see was crackling snow, but I could make out the dialogue. Occasionally an airplane would fly overhead and the picture would miraculously appear for a second. It was exciting to see what the voices I had heard actually looked like. I asked Roy why he didn't put an antennae up or get cable. He said he didn't watch TV much, and when he did, he knew what was going on without looking at the screen, so why bother? After that week, I didn't watch much either. I helped him in the shop.

I dusted and cleaned, transforming the shop so significantly in just a couple of days that Roy began paying me a salary of $75 a week. I had never had so much money! I was supposed to go to Northern Illinois in Dekalb in the fall, but I was planning on telling my mother that I had changed my mind. I liked my life with Roy, our little mom-and-pop operation of magic and fortune telling. I didn't think Mom would mind. She hadn't even saved enough for the whole first year, so we would have to pay for the rest by loans. I asked Roy what he thought. He said that whatever I wanted was fine. If I wanted to stay. If I wanted to go. It was my decision.

The store's street traffic was negligible, mostly teenagers who came to look or buy Voodoo candles or crystals. His main clients were old Mexican and Polish women who grew to love me. ("Such fine hips for childbearing." "All he needed was a good woman to get this place cleaned up." "Do you have the gift of sight, too?")

I didn't see my father every time we had sex, but almost. I told Roy about it and he nodded.

"I'm not surprised. Most people think the dead are closest to their loved ones when they are seriously ill or dying. Yet, short of actual death, it is actually sex that brings them closest. The better the climax, the more likely the connection. Hell, sometimes when I get off, there's so many dead folk standing around that I feel like I'm doing a sex show in a fucking grave yard!"

Then he laughed and patted my head.

"Nothing to be ashamed of, Coco Bean. Sex, life, death, food. They're all good. They fit together. Though to live in America in this century you'd never know it."

When Roy did house calls or healing massages, I stood behind the counter. When he worked the counter, I went up and down the halls reading the articles that plastered his walls. Most were tabloid stories about near-death experiences and contacts with the spirit world. ("I like the authentic ones best," he told me. I was glad he wasn't a fraud.) There were some creepy ones about mercy-killing doctors and nurses. Quite a few about psychics who had found the graves of murder victims. Others were about funerals in distant places. The Day of the Dead in Mexico. Burning funeral pyres in India. But most were accounts of people who had crossed over and returned. I loved to read those. I felt they gave me a clue about my father. Only a small portion of the articles had nothing to do with death or the life beyond. Either people I assumed Roy knew or important moments in history—he had the moon walk and Nixon's resignation.

It must have been mid July before I found the article about Roy himself. It was short, plastered in the most out of the way place, under a window sill so that the top of his head in the photo curled up under the sill. He didn't have a beard then and his hair was shorter. It said that he had been released on murder charges because there wasn't enough evidence to hold him. The clipping was from an upstate New York paper, where I knew Roy had lived many years ago. Roy was described as a "self-proclaimed psychic who catered primarily to elderly women." The victim was "Eleanor Spearman, an 82-year-old widow who had worked for the telephone company for 33 years and had no surviving relatives." True, Roy was weird, but he was also gentle and kind. He would never kill anyone. It would have been an insult to ask him about the story. It was natural that if most of your clients were elderly, some were going to die.

Roy was good to me. He was the first person to talk openly to me about suicide. He told me that there were places in the world where it was actually the most honorable way to die. And one night when he held me naked in bed, stroking me as if I were a tiny kitten, he told me that the type of pain my father must have suffered was too great for him to go on living, that his death was actually an act of love toward me because he would have been a horrible father if he had lived. Then Roy ran his hand along my ribs, like he was strumming a guitar, and said, "Hey, you know what, Coco Bean, you're losing weight."

* * *

In August, I was reading an astrology book when Roy said he had to go out. He had a house call with Mrs. Antozek. She usually came on Friday with her two friends, Mrs. Solski and Mrs. Bonavich, but Roy said she wasn't feeling well and wouldn't be able to come on Friday.

"Should be back in a couple of hours, Coco Bean," he said and patted me on the head. It was a Wednesday; I remember now because of what happened later that week. I was feeling great. My clothing had become baggy. Roy didn't have a scale but I imagined I had lost about twenty pounds. I felt lighter, and I could no longer grab the roll of fat around my middle with my hand. If I had still planned on college, I would have needed new clothes. Mom would be relieved that she wouldn't have to buy me any. I hadn't told her I wasn't going yet and was dreading the event, so I was stocking up on as many positives about the situation as possible to present to her.

As usual, we had very few customers that afternoon. I read the entire book. I wanted to learn more about astrology. If I didn't have the gift, I could at least contribute to the business by doing charts.

Roy got home around six and we walked to Devon for Indian food. He was ravenous that night. He had three curry dishes—one chicken and two beef—deep-fried pastry filled with cheese, sag paneer, a large stack of nan, and a vat of rice. His finger tips were oily from handling so much. I loved Indian, but I stuck with just the tandoori chicken, no rice or nan—I liked that I was losing weight. I was thinking about the possibility of actually buying a bathing suit and going to Montrose beach on the weekend. I hadn't been since grade school.

On Friday morning, Mrs. Solski and Mrs. Bonavich came in by themselves. They were both shorter than me and stocky as tree trunks, with heavy breasts and wide ankles. Instead of wearing their usual flowered housedresses, they both wore black.

"I'm sorry to hear about Mrs. Antozek," I said.

"Thank you, dearie. I wish I could say we grow used to it by now, but it's still a shock," said Mrs. Solski. Mrs. Bonavich uttered a little, muffled cry.

"I'm sure she'll feel better soon," I said.

Mrs. Solski drew her face back, perplexed.

"In heaven, you mean?"

"Wait, you mean . . ."

"I'm sorry, I thought you knew. She's dead. They found her body yesterday. All dressed up, like she was getting ready to go out but had needed a rest first. Peaceful in her bed. I called about our appointment today and her son answered. He hadn't been able to get her on the phone since Tuesday. The funeral is tomorrow. And your Roy, he predicted it. He knew. He told her it would be before the end of the summer so she had time to get everything in order."

I remained perfectly still. I could feel the opening of the hollow hole, myself falling backwards, but I fought it. No, it couldn't be. Not Roy. He had the gift, that was all. He was a gentle man. If you worked with elderly people, it was inevitable that some were going to die. If I hadn't seen the article about the woman in New York, such a thought would never have entered my mind.

"I'll get Roy," I said.

On Saturday, I told Roy I had to go shopping for school clothes. I didn't ask my mom to contribute. I used money I had saved from working for Roy, holding out just enough cash to go to the pawn shop and retrieve my clarinet in the red velvet case. At the end of the month, I went to DeKalb as planned, telling Roy I would call him at Thanksgiving. I didn't, nor did I call Benny or any of the others. I hadn't seen much of them since I moved in with Roy anyway. By Thanksgiving I was forty pounds lighter than I had been when I graduated from high school, and I was going to make the Dean's list. I knew I would never be thin or beautiful, but I could be happy. At spring break, my mother told me that Mark had stopped by and left his phone number. This news made me smile. But I didn't call him either. I was not looking back. I had seen the face of my father, and I could leave my past behind.

* * *

It wasn't until my junior year that I woke in the middle of the night and knew: Roy had killed Mrs. Antozek, he had killed the woman in New York as well, and probably many others. He had known Mrs. Antozek wasn't coming on Friday even though her friends hadn't. He had told me the Wednesday he went to see her, yet I had dismissed it. In fact, I had dismissed much more than that one detail; his culpability had been present in every aspect of what he did and what he said when I lived with him. The articles pasted on his walls. The way he talked about death. Why hadn't I asked him about his own release on murder charges? Why had I suddenly decided to go to college? Because I hadn't wanted to know—and I knew Roy would not lie to me if confronted. But I had known, *did know*, as clearly as I had seen my father's face when Roy and I made love. As I sat in my skinny single bed in the dorm room I shared with my friend Vicky, I knew. And I knew I would turn Roy in if I had to—I couldn't be complicit in the next death—but I wanted to at least see him first. I felt I owed him that.

I woke Vicky, borrowed her car, and drove to Chicago in the dead of night. I pulled up in front of Roy's shop before daybreak. A trace of pink was leaking across the sky. I held my breath as I opened the car door. The tilting of the building had reached a treacherous extreme, but the building itself was empty—windows boarded over, great sheets of paint curling away from the surrounding wood. A sign posted a few feet in front of the door announced the coming of luxury condos. I stood for a moment on the sidewalk and looked at the building where I had spent the summer before college, where I had seen my father, and then I got right back in my friend's car and headed for DeKalb. As I drove to the freeway, I watched the sun rise through my windshield. A swirl of dark clouds moving against the red sky made me think for a moment of Roy's flushed face and dark beard the first time we made love, and then the configuration drifted and faded as quickly as it had formed.

Across a Great Distance

Kerrie sorted through the mail looking for a letter she was expecting from her pen pal, Sonja, in Holland. Kerrie had settled on Sonja because Sonja had expressed a preference for "snail mail." Kerrie was the only student in her seventh-grade class who didn't want to exchange e-mails. When Jonathan Swartz had laughed, calling her "pioneer girl," she had retorted with, "It is called *pen* pal, techno-nerd." That had shut him up. Now, a year later, she was the only one from the class who still corresponded with her pen pal.

Kerrie loved the idea that she could drop a piece of mail in the blue receptacle at the end of her street—just a metal box on four legs—and ten days later the envelope would arrive over the ocean in the door slot of a girl who lived in a tall skinny house facing a canal in Amsterdam. Kerrie liked to close her eyes and picture the vastness of the ocean. She had never actually seen it, but she had flown over Lake Michigan once and had been amazed at the size of the rippling gray sheet of water. E-mail was too much like turning on a light switch, convenient, but not as mysterious or romantic as candles.

The heavy stack of mail contained a few catalogues—which Kerrie would take to her room and flip through later—but mostly invoices, solicitations, and business-type items for her parents. She paused when she came to a thick hand-addressed letter to her father. Kerrie placed the rest of the stack on the dining room table and stared at the envelope. "Danny," it said in tight black script, and then, in entirely different handwriting, his last name, "Doyle," and address in blue ink. In the upper left hand corner was the message, "sorry—I should have sent this before—Y." No actual address, though the brief apology was written in three lines, the same way a return name and address would be written. Big, blue, loopy script. Feminine writing.

Sometimes Kerrie's mother received personal mail, but Kerrie could not recall coming across a hand-addressed letter to her father—even on his birthday. Both his parents and his older brother were dead. He did have a sister living out west and a few cousins but they weren't close. And the return address made it even odder. "Sorry"? And Y. Who was Y? Kerrie put the letter down and picked up the stack to continue sorting. Near the bottom was the letter she had been looking for from Sonja. Seeing it—the foreign stamps, the neat slanting script—did not imbue her with the same sense of excitement it usually did. The letter to her father had captured the part of her brain with capacity for anticipation and wonder. Still, she had hope that reading Sonja's letter would rekindle her interest in her pen pal's news.

Kerrie left the rest of the mail on the table and trotted upstairs to her bedroom to read her letter at the privacy of her purple desk. Her whole room was purple, yellow, and red. Her older sister Lisa's room had a pink and white color scheme, which made it easier to purchase accessories. Stores carried plenty of white furniture and fabrics. Kerrie had had to paint her desk herself, but she loved the contrast of the purple against her supplies—her red sealing wax, her sunflower stationary, and her yellow lamp. Lisa called it gaudy, but Kerrie just laughed; she knew Lisa recognized her flair for assembly. Besides, she didn't think pink and white accurately reflected Lisa. Kerrie believed that people should be honest about who they were to the world by the physical ways in which they presented themselves. Lisa was a jock; pink and white was too girlish for her.

When unfolded, Sonja's letter looked as inviting as it always did. Three pale blue pages, three neat paragraphs per page. Her slanted script so perfect and even that it looked like a personal form of stylized calligraphy. Kerrie's soul mate from across the sea! Yet no matter how hard Kerrie tried, she could not lose herself in the letter the way she usually did. She skimmed the first paragraph—the one that customarily asked about Kerrie's health, life, and family—in order to reach the second paragraph about Peter. He was the boy Sonja had liked for the last three letters in a row. But Kerrie couldn't concentrate. The envelope to her father beckoned. How could she find interest in Sonja's letter when something far more mysterious resided on the dining room table? Who was Y? And why had a different person addressed the letter from the one who wrote "Danny"? When Kerrie was younger she sometimes wrote the name of her mother's mother on the envelope of a thank-you note, and afterwards her mother would fill in the address. But both sets of writing on the letter to her father were clearly adult. If anything, the black writing seemed more solid and mature. Could that person have been too old and sick to write the entire address?

Kerrie turned her attention back to Sonja's letter. Sonja was worried that Peter had a crush on her best friend, Lisel. Sonja had found out that they had talked on the phone twice at night. Kerrie was secretly glad because she felt that she and Sonja were best friends and Lisel's betrayal would make that fact more evident to Sonja. Kerrie had never even met Sonja but was jealous that Sonja had a flesh and blood friend whom she liked better. Kerrie knew that jealousy was a character flaw, so she was happy that she could feel less jealous. As she read further, she learned that Peter claimed he had called Lisel to ask what he should get Sonja for her birthday, but her birthday was over a month away. Sonja asked Kerrie what she thought of this.

Sonja's letter concluded, as they both always ended their letters, with a quick critique of the most recent novel she had read. It was a way of signaling what they both saw as their commitment to their development as junior intellectuals.

Maybe the letter to her father was from a mistress? A lover who hadn't had enough nerve to put it in the mail so her friend, Y, had done it for her. Or worse, maybe a jealous friend had taken a letter the lover was contemplating giving him and gone ahead and put it in the mail without the lover's knowledge. Kerrie's mother was due home soon—what if she opened the letter? Kerrie pushed back her chair so quickly that it wobbled on its back legs and would have toppled if Kerrie hadn't caught it before she dashed from the room. She had to get the letter before her mother saw it! She would wait until Lisa got home from school and they would decide together what to do with the strange missive.

* * *

When Angie got home from the library she was happy to see her daughters, Lisa and Kerrie, making a salad together in the kitchen. She could smell the left-over meat loaf in the oven.

"Well, this is a pleasant surprise," said Angie as she hung her keys on the hook by the back door, a Mother's Day plaque that Kerrie had made in first grade. It had two buttons for eyes, a hook for a nose, and two hooks for ears. At the time, Angie had been surprised that her teacher would allow an entire class of six and seven-year-olds to make gifts that involved so many sharp hooks, but no one had been injured and the plaque had come in handy over the years. Danny could be absent-minded, and without a place to hang his keys he inevitably lost them.

"You were late, so we thought we would just get started," said Lisa. "We put the meatloaf in to reheat. I hope that's okay,"

"That's great," said Angie.

"When's Dad getting home?" asked Kerrie.

"He's on his way. He called on the cell as I was leaving."

"Why don't you go rest or something and we'll just finish dinner," said Lisa. Angie started to make a joke—about where her real daughters were—but changed her mind; the girls so seldom did things together anymore that she shouldn't make them feel uneasy about pitching in together. Angie had come from a large Italian family, Danny from a surprisingly small Catholic family, half Polish, half Irish. Both Angie and Danny had wanted a large family—Angie to duplicate hers, Danny to compensate for his.

Because they had gotten a late start, they considered themselves lucky to squeeze out two daughters before the doctor had told them it was too risky to have more. Yet as her children grew, they seemed so different from each other that it was more like two kids from different families residing in the same house. Angie worried that once they were grown and didn't have her around anymore to bind them, they would drift even further apart.

Lisa was big boned, like Angie's side of the family, but fair like Danny's. Lisa was practical and hearty, a sports fan who played softball in the summer, soccer in the fall, and basketball in the winter. Kerrie was lean like Danny and dark like Angie's family. She was more whimsical, more temperamental, more social, though also bookish—actively working on becoming an eccentric. In the winter she wore a purple beret and a funny fake fur coat that looked different from the kinds the other girls wore. If it were the seventies, she might have been a hippie; in the fifties she certainly would have been a beatnik. Though if Kerrie wanted, she probably could become a beauty queen. Kerrie could no more sit through a football game with Danny and Lisa than Angie could.

Lately Kerrie had become dismissive of the rest of her family, particularly her father and Lisa, whom she seemed to consider rubes unable to understand her sophistication.

Angie left the girls to their work while she went to the dining room to sort the mail. She quickly flipped through it. Nothing of interest. Before she placed the pile on the sideboard to give the girls a clean table to set, she paused to smile at the sound of them whispering in the kitchen, happy that they shared a secret. She knew that whatever they said, it couldn't be too serious—Lisa was in one piece, no injuries, Kerrie was too young to be pregnant, and the house was still standing, no signs of damage anywhere.

Angie kicked off her shoes and padded upstairs to change into slacks. Her calves and feet ached from wearing high heels. Usually she wore flats, but today there had been a lunch for a potential large donor to the library. She felt she had needed to dress to impress, something she didn't do often.

* * *

Kerrie had wanted to open the letter, determine a course of action based on the contents. If it was another woman and the letter wasn't a "Dear John," perhaps she and Lisa could go see the woman, appeal to her sense of decency. Lisa had scoffed at that.

"Dad having an affair? Are you crazy? Think about it?"

Kerrie admitted the scenario was unlikely, but half the affairs she had seen in movies or read about in novels were unlikely. And though their father didn't look particularly attractive to either of them, they were incapable of knowing what a woman his own age would think of him. He hadn't lost his hair or grown fat like a lot of their friends' fathers. Sure, he was quiet, introspective, but a lot of women liked that. It was family legend the way their mother had made both the first move and the second. He was a college student who came regularly to the library where she worked. She was five years his senior. On one occasion when he seemed to be absent-mindedly staring at her, she walked over to his table and said, "Just because I'm a librarian doesn't mean that I have to look like one." He blushed. "Or act like one," she added and turned on her heels back to the information desk.

He didn't come in for several weeks after that, but when he did, their mother straight-out asked him for a date.

"Maybe Mom is too bossy for him or he decided he wanted a younger woman."

"Give me a break. Don't be ridiculous. Dad would never cheat on Mom. He wouldn't even know how to meet a woman unless Mom helped him," said Lisa, but, from the furrow in her brow, Kerrie knew Lisa was growing less certain. She was the type of person who stated as fact things she wanted to be true in the hope that verbalizing would make them more likely. "Besides, even if there was something to your theory, we need to give Dad a chance to handle it on his own. Why don't we put the letter on Dad's dresser? That way he'll know that *someone* knew it wasn't ordinary mail. He won't know if it was us or Mom."

Before their mother got home, they had put the envelope on his dresser. Their parents had identical dressers on opposite sides of their small master suite. After their mother arrived, as they made dinner, they whispered about the possibilities.

"Who do we know whose name starts with the letter 'Y'?" asked Kerrie.

"The Yudkowskis down the street."

"Yuck! Dad would never have an affair with Mrs. Yudkowski."

They named half a dozen possibilities before Lisa came up with the idea of their Aunt Yolunda.

Kerrie turned the idea over in her mind.

"We never even met her. Of course that could make sense. If Dad is having an affair with her, he wouldn't want a family get-together. It would be kind of awkward. And it's not like she's a blood relative."

"She's bigger than Dad," said Lisa. "I saw her next to him in a photo."

This had been a problem for Lisa in finding a boyfriend.

"Mom's not exactly small. And Mom said Yolunda is her opposite—real quiet—more like Dad. Maybe she and Dad have some sort of weird bond, her being the widow of Dad's brother and all that."

"The way your mind works." Lisa sighed. "He died before we were even born."

"Yeah, still, you've got to admit, it's a possibility."

"No," said Lisa, but it sounded more like yes.

They were quiet while they walked around the dining room table, placing folded napkins and flatware. The kitchen had a door, so they had been able to talk while getting the food together. They didn't know how much of what they said in the dining room carried upstairs. They both looked up startled when they heard their father come in the back door. As he entered the dining room, Kerrie felt she was seeing him for the first time in a long time as a man who did not simply vaporize into the incomprehensible world of business when he left each morning.

"Where's your mother?"

"Upstairs," they said in unison, frozen with flatware in their hands, like culinary statues. Would he find the letter now as he emptied his spare change into the glass brandy snifter he kept on his dresser for such a purpose? Before he changed into his sweat shirt and sweat pants? Or after? Had they propped up the envelope sufficiently among all the clutter of the dresser top? Would he crumple it in a ball or open the letter in front of their mother? Would he confess?

They didn't move until they heard his athletic trot ascend to the top of the stairs and heard him open his bedroom door.

"We should have thrown it out," whispered Kerrie.

"No," said Lisa. "It's not up to us—we don't even know for sure what it is." Her words reopened the debate: what was in the letter? They returned to the kitchen where they didn't need to whisper. Lisa laughed, more nervously than Kerrie had ever heard her.

"Maybe the letter isn't anything—just a bill that went to the wrong house, the Yudkowski's, and they only now got around to sticking it in an envelope and putting it in the mail."

"It was pretty thick."

"A couple of bills?"

Hope of this pedestrian possibility was dashed when their parents didn't bound down the stairs the way they usually did after changing out of their work clothes. Lisa arranged the sliced meatloaf on a platter and Kerrie tossed the salad. When they had everything on the table, Lisa went to the bottom of the stairs and called up, "Mom, Dad, dinner's ready. You coming?"

A full minute passed before the door to their parents' room opened and their mother stuck her head out.

"Just start without us."

This command was without precedent; the two of them eating alone at the dining room table with their parents upstairs. Most nights they ate as a family at the dining room table. Dinner around the table was a formality their mother insisted upon unless their parents were going out or they all had an event they needed to get to quickly. Then they might have pizza or sandwiches in the kitchen. Never just the two of them at the dining room table.

"We should have made potatoes or rice or something," said Lisa as they sat down.

Kerrie popped back up and went to the kitchen, returning with a bag of Doritos. She poured a stack of chips on Lisa's plate.

"I wouldn't want you to try to survive a night without some starch. Particularly when our family is in the middle of falling apart."

"You don't have to be such a jerk. Besides, when did you become the big protector of this family?" Lisa clearly didn't want to reach for a chip, but couldn't resist. "This is all just a big fantasy. Speculation. We don't even know for sure that Dad is having an affair."

"We know," said Kerrie. "Whether you're ready to admit it is another matter."

Kerrie placed the bag in the center of the table so that she, too, could snack from it while they ate. The meatloaf tasted dry in her mouth. They had reheated it for too long. And she had put too much dressing on the salad. Soggy. She ate mostly chips. They both did. Neither spoke. Usually their mother asked questions while they ate.

Kerrie considered apologizing for her remark about the starch. Lisa was right. She didn't need to be a jerk. Lisa's weight problem wasn't her fault. Kerrie didn't actually eat any less; she just had a better metabolism. Before she could speak, they heard their parents' door open above them, and then, from the rhythm of the steps, recognized the sound of their mother hurrying downstairs.

"Where's Dad?" asked Lisa when their mother appeared. She had the same worry furrow between her eye brows that Lisa had. The stress on their mother's face was evident; her lips were pursed and her eyes were rimmed in red but her skin didn't appear puffy or swollen from crying. Her posture was actually more determined than sad or angry. "I need my address book. I think I left it by the kitchen phone last night. Your Aunt Yolunda's number."

Kerrie looked at Lisa. Their mother disappeared into the kitchen. A half-chewed Dorito chip caught in Kerrie's throat, a sharp bridge between the soft membrane walls. She took a big swallow of milk, felt the liquid bubble up in her throat, thought she was going to choke, spit milk across the table, when, miraculously, the chip dislodged.

"Are you okay?" asked Lisa.

Kerrie could manage no more than an affirmative nod. She felt a surprising surge of tenderness toward Lisa for showing concern.

Their mother emerged from the kitchen, clutching the worn green address book, bulging with envelopes and notes containing addresses she hadn't yet transferred.

She didn't even remark on the bag of Doritos as she passed the table headed for the stairs. After dinner, Kerrie and Lisa cleared the table, scraped the dishes, and loaded the dishwasher without arguing about whose turn it was.

* * *

Danny had just opened his hand to release his spare change when he noticed the envelope. His heart paused. He didn't hear the coins clatter into the snifter. He had been thinking about his brother all day. For the first year after his brother's suicide, he thought about Jake constantly. During that year, he felt as if Jake was sitting on his shoulder, weighing down his right side. The next few years, Jake moved from sitting on his shoulder to hovering above it a couple of times a day, then a few times a week—at least consciously. When the children were born, Jake faded even more. Yet Jake never vanished entirely. He simply moved from the shoulder to a chair in the far back of Danny's brain, a silent partner who announced himself in moments of uncertainty or stress. Today Danny had gotten the word that he was going to have to choose two managers to lay off. He knew who the two least productive were, the two least competent—he also knew that both of these people had families, mortgages—and he knew that there were always consequences. The lay-offs might be the beginning of a chain of ripple effects for these people; worrying about where those chains would lead had set Danny to thinking about Jake. What had set *him* off? What had started the chain that ended with a bullet in his brain? Now this: a letter with his name so clearly printed in Jake's tight, controlled script that it was almost as if Jake had responded in writing to Danny's thoughts, as if the piece of mail had fallen directly from heaven to his dresser top. Danny picked up the envelope, standard business sized, cheap, faded with age, though not yellow, simply off-white, fat enough to contain a half dozen folded pages.

"Angie, where did this come from?" His wife reclined backwards on the bed, in just her camisole and panties, her head at the foot, her bare legs propped up so that her heels rested on the headboard. She swiveled around to rise, planted her feet on the floor, and crossed the short alley between the bed and his dresser to look over his shoulder.

"What is it? One of the girls must have brought it up for you."

"Jake. This is Jake's handwriting."

"*Noooo*, it can't be," said Angie, snatching the letter from his hand. "How do you know? Are you sure? It looks like two different people's handwriting."

Danny didn't respond.

"Are you going to open it? It's probably nothing. You think it's nothing?"

"They never found a note," said Danny as he sank back on the bed. Angie sat beside him. Danny slipped the tip of his thumb under a bubble in the seal, planning to tear the fold open. Before he could, the seal cracked, like the spit of his dead brother was too ancient and brittle to do anything except break in response to a human touch.

* * *

Danny and Jake hadn't been in regular touch at the time of the suicide. They were in an unspoken feud that had started a few years earlier when their mother's will had been read. Their parents had owned so little that it seemed impossible that the disposal of their property could create any problems. Yet the bequeathing of their final assets was absurd. Danny was certain that in their unsophisticated world, they didn't understand the unfairness. Danny and Jake's sister, Catherine, had been given the furniture; Danny got the car and the insubstantial savings account; and Jake got the house. It was only a modest Chicago bungalow, too far west of Ashland to have much value, particularly at that time. But the place was worth far more than Danny and Catherine's inheritances combined. Danny understood his parents' logic (for the will was written long before his father died)—Jake, as the oldest and married son, should inherit the castle. Danny, a bachelor, still footloose, could use transportation and a little cash; and Catherine was a girl. Danny was willing to let the imbalance go. Catherine was not. She was outraged. She wanted to combine everything, sell all their parents' belongings at auction, and split the proceeds three ways—equally. When Jake refused, said he was going to live in the house, Catherine cut him off entirely. Both of them were annoyed at Danny for not completely denouncing the other. Catherine and Jake never spoke again. Catherine didn't even attend his funeral.

The last time Danny saw Jake was before Danny married Angie and moved out from Chicago to Lombard. Danny had gone out to their parents' former house to tell Jake that he and Angie were getting married, had already bought a house in Lombard. At the front door, Yolunda told Danny that Jake and some friends were out back in the garage that he had converted to a sound and composing studio. The grass in the back yard was overgrown and weedy—so different from the neat green square their father had sweated over— and the studio was thick with marijuana smoke.

Jake lay draped across an old mattress. Reggie, a friend of Jake's from their high school garage band days, and a guy Danny didn't know sat propped against the walls, their legs sprawled out in front of them. It seemed as if Jake were holding court. No one rose or even nodded in Danny's direction, though Jake did pause in his dissertation to say, "Hey, man, pull up a pillow." Danny sank onto an unoccupied pillow against the wall next to the door, his legs sticking straight out in front of him so that he felt like a stiff wooden doll or a puppet.

Jake continued talking, stopping every now and then to consider a response. Danny tried to connect phrases but the new way Jake and his friends discussed music sounded like a foreign language to him.

"It's an organized pattern of sounds that keeps . . ."

"No, if music functions as sound effects, it has a *disorganized* quality that . . ."

"Combined sounds create the dominant image . . ."

"No way, stopping a soundtrack makes just as big an impact . . ."

Danny had never been as talented or as driven as Jake. In fact, he had only stayed in music as long as he had because of Jake.

"But if you interrupt field recordings with electronic sounds . . ."

"No, that's the whole point, you need to punctuate to give a sense of space . . ."

Then Jake said something Danny had heard him say many times, a phrase that had sounded profound to Danny the first time he had heard the words.

"It's about how you move the air. That's all sound is—the way you move the air."

Now Danny recognized the words as a standard line of Jake's, a line he used to stop conversation, dismiss the weight of what everyone else said. Apparently Jake felt he was losing the argument. It seemed like the right moment for Danny to say what he had come to say. He considered asking Jake to step outside so that they could speak in private, except such a request seemed too dramatic. So he just dove in.

"Jake, I have some news."

The room grew quiet at his interruption.

"Angie and I are getting married. We bought a place out in Lombard."

"That's cool," said Jake, but the shift of his eyes and lack of questions said otherwise. The two men against the walls mumbled congratulatory words.

"This calls for a toast," said Jake, retrieving a half-smoked joint and a book of matches from the ashtray without bothering to sit up. "Or should I say a toke."

"No, no thanks," said Danny. He already felt like Beaver Cleaver cast into a den of thieves; his refusal to smoke exacerbated the situation. Danny had stopped getting high a while back. The decision wasn't made on moral grounds, just a lack of interest. Being stoned wasn't as fun now that he had a regular job to get up for every morning. Besides, Angie didn't really approve. He might have made an exception this once, but he was meeting Angie and her parents for dinner later to make wedding plans.

"No dope. A corporate job. Marrying a librarian. Moving out to status symbol land. Where are you going for the honeymoon—Niagara Falls?"

They all laughed, including Danny, though he knew it was more than playful teasing. The remark was laden with aggression.

Later, Jake called to say he couldn't make the wedding, big recording gig. Though Danny said he understood, he didn't. He got two calls from Jake the week before the suicide; Danny planned to return them, though first he wanted to make Jake sweat a little. Then it was too late.

* * *

Danny read the letter aloud to Angie. It began by talking about a woman named Kay, a woman Jake claimed he was in love with, couldn't live without. He wanted Danny to call her, tell her about the suicide, tell her that Jake still loved her. Without any transition the subject changed to Jake's music, how unfairly he had been treated, how he wasn't as recognized as he should be, as he had expected to be at this time in his life. A rejection he had received from some producer. Then the letter disintegrated into musical notes, as if he were talking in notes, using the notes as words. Then back to Kay. Then a stream-of-consciousness mumble-jumble about their childhood, their parents, the house, Catherine, their first bicycles. And then ending with those familiar words…the ones about everything having to do with "how we move the air."

"This doesn't make any sense," said Danny.

"It never did," said Angie.

The letter returned to Kay, her husband who didn't appreciate her. Then the house, how Danny and Catherine could have it now that he was gone. Yolunda and his daughter could move in with Yolunda's mother. Then Kay again, a phone number where Danny could reach her. The letter ended without any closure or signature. To Danny's surprise, there was no mention of the two phone calls Danny never returned. Danny had always thought that his lack of response was a primary factor in Jake's suicide.

"I'm going to call Yolunda," said Angie. "We need to know when she found this."

Angie pulled on her sweat pants and a t-shirt and left the room. Danny reread the letter, searching for a clue or pattern, until Angie returned a few minutes later with her address book. As Danny stood over her, she sat at the head of the bed next to the telephone table, her eyes darting back and forth between the book and the phone as she punched out the number.

"What are the girls doing?"

"Eating Doritos . . . hello, Yolunda, it's Angie, Danny got the letter . . ." Before Angie could say more she appeared to be silenced by Yolunda's onslaught of explanation. Long stretches of silence were followed by brief acknowledgments and questions. "Ah-huh, ah-huh. Why? Ah-huh. Yes, of course. When did you find it? No. No. Don't worry. Ah-huh. Ah-huh. No. Yeah. I see. I understand. Yes. Nothing really . . . no, mostly he just rambles about music . . . no, no . . . that's okay . . . yes, soon . . . And Yo, thanks."

Angie gently replaced the receiver.

"When did she find it?"

"The night he died." Her voice was soft. "She had it all this time. She never opened it. All these years the letter has been in the back of a drawer."

"Huh? What's going on? Why didn't she send it before?" Angie shrugged.

"She was too embarrassed to show it to anyone because he didn't leave a letter to her. She *says* that now she's trying to get her life in order—move on. I hope that's true—it's about time."

Danny sank down next to Angie.

"He doesn't even mention that I didn't return his calls."

"I know," said Angie. "He barely even mentions Yolunda."

They were both quiet while Danny changed his clothes. Angie remained on the bed.

"Are you going to try to find this Kay?" asked Angie.

"I don't think so," said Danny. "After all these years, why does she need this creeping back in her life? Maybe she's convinced herself she didn't have anything to do with it."

"She didn't. It was Jake. All Jake."

Danny rejoined her on the bed. They both leaned back from their bent knees until their spines were pressed against the made bed. They clasped hands and stared blankly at the ceiling. Angie clicked off the bedside lamp. The street light illuminated the room just enough so that they could make out the hazy shapes of the furniture, as if they were pointillist paintings rather than solid objects.

"Are you going to tell Catherine?"

"Not the part about the house. It's Yolunda's house now."

"It probably wouldn't hold up in court anyway."

"It's ironic; by giving the house to their eldest son, my parents actually gave it to Yolunda, who they never really liked."

"Everything is ironic," said Angie. "Everything we say or do."

"My parents would have liked you." He laughed. "They wouldn't have understood you, but they would have liked you."

Over the next hour, they spoke only when they couldn't keep a thought inside. There was little point, since nothing either of them thought required an answer. A pure and gentle moment—a short period when they both understood there were no real answers and neither of them minded. Danny thought about the dismissive way Jake had said sound was all about the way you moved the air. That was actually all that life itself was about. Moving air, into your lungs and out again. It was as simple as that. Jake had decided to stop the air.

At nine, Angie said she had better make sure that the girls were doing their homework or getting ready for bed.

* * *

Shortly after Kerrie changed into her pajamas, she heard her father emerge from her parents' bedroom and descend the stairs for a late night dinner in the kitchen with her mother. She had imagined her father had waited until they were all in their rooms because he was too ashamed to face them. Kerrie was not worried about her parents breaking up. She had faith in her mother's strength and pragmatism. Kerrie was sure that her mother had either given her father a directive to end his relationship with Yolunda or had done it herself. Why else could she have needed her phone number? Her father loved her mother, and her mother loved her father. She would forgive him; her mother was not the hysterical type. Their family would remain intact.

Though Kerrie wasn't supposed to light matches in her room unless she asked permission, Kerrie lit the large purple candle on her desk and started her response to Sonja's letter. She liked the smell of lavender and the romance of writing by candlelight. Her first paragraph, like Sonja's, burst with pleasantries and questions about Sonja's life. Then she told Sonja her story:

A terrible thing happened in my family tonight. We found out that my father was having an affair with our Aunt Yolunda. She is the widow of my father's brother who died a mysterious death. My mother is a brave woman who called our aunt and put an end to it. Someday you will meet my father and think it weird that he had an affair. He is a good man but you can never really know another person can you? Even your own father. All of our parents had lives before us that we will never know but I found out a part of my father's tonight. I think my father probably felt sorry for my aunt because she was a young widow. He probably thought that he should go over to her house and help and one thing led to another. That is life. It is so weird. Please don't tell this to anyone. It is a big secret I am telling only you because you are such a vast distance away and do not know anyone my family knows. Also I trust you. I think you might even be my best friend because I can say things to you on paper that I could not tell anyone aloud. It is so weird like I am writing a letter to the inside of me.

As for Peter you should put your foot down hard like my mother did. If Lisel does not like it she is not a real friend to begin with. I hope hearing about my family helps you know this. Write soon!!!

Luv, Kera (by the way I am changing my name)

My Real Name Is Charles

I'm going to try not to lie. That's why I told you my real name. Charles. Charles Francis O'Rourke. I know the form I filled out says Carlos Ortiz, but I want to be truthful here. That's why I'm telling you my real name. Charlie to the dudes who knew me back in the day. Everyone in Chicago knows me as Carlos, but the people who know me out in Elmhurst call me Charlie. Elmhurst is where I grew up. We moved from the south side to the suburbs when I was about four. The house was just as small as the one in Chicago, a yellow brick bungalow, but they got more trees out in the burbs. My parents still live there. My younger brothers, Jimmy and Desmond, moved to the east coast after they finished college. I have one sister, Mary, who still lives in Elmhurst, only a few blocks from our folks. An all-American Irish Catholic family.

Okay. Okay. Okay.

I really want to cut down on lying. At least when it's not necessary. I guess it's kind of an occupational hazard. Heh. Heh. When you have to lie about some things, it becomes easy to lie about everything else. You start to tell the truth, and, well, it just seems to spin off in a more interesting direction. It comes more naturally than the truth. That's one of the reasons I'm here, right?

On the phone, you said you couldn't tell anyone what I said here unless I was suicidal, homicidal, or abusing kids. Well, I sure ain't homicidal or suicidal and I don't have no kids. And it wouldn't matter if I did; I'd never hurt a flea. So, like I said, there are times when I have to lie, but I'm going to try to tell the truth here. And it starts with my name. It does say Carlos Ortiz on my driver's license—at least the one I use most of the time in Chicago. The one with Charles O'Rourke on it has my parents' Elmhurst address. I have a third one too—I hardly ever use it, just for emergencies—but

I don't think I'll tell you my name on that one. What's the point? It's enough that I told you it exists, that I've told you the truth. The details don't matter none. It's not like the name on that one has any real significance. I'll just say it was issued in Texas.

Okay, okay. I'm getting to that.

I started using Carlos over twenty years ago at a party. Everyone was high and these two guys were doing a Cheech and Chong imitation. One of them called me Carlos. It got a big laugh. My hair was solid black back then—black Irish my grandmother used to call me—and I had a black Fu Manchu mustache. The name just kind of stuck. I can do a pretty good Mexican accent when I try. And I've been south of the border plenty of times, that's for sure. So I just started telling people I grew up in Juarez. No one has ever questioned it. I know the town pretty well.

So I guess by now you think you've figured out what I do. Well, I'm not a drug dealer if that's what you think—I just sell pot. Marijuana. Less dangerous than alcohol. Less addictive. To be honest, I used to sell more than pot, back in the late sixties, early seventies, when people were experimenting with everything. I admit it. I sold whatever I could get my hands on. By the eighties, I had cut way back. I invested a lot of my profits. I own a three flat, two game rooms, and my own home. Or I should say the bank owns them. I own the mortgages. Heh. Heh. I was able to stake some pretty hefty down payments. I was always good at math. If I had stayed in college, I probably would have gone into some type of high finance or investments. But I was lured by the street. You know what they say—can't beat the street. Or is it can't compete with the street? It was the times, you know. I graduated from high school in sixty-seven. Strange times.

Me?

No way, dude, I don't use. I still smoke a little grass, prefer it really to booze. Just pot. I'm not saying I *never* do any coke, but rarely. I mean it would be dishonest to say "I use coke" when you do it as infrequently as I do. I did an eight ball—oh, I don't know—a month or so ago. But I can't even remember the last time before that that I did more than a short line. No way, I'm strictly pot. Mary-jo-wana. I've seen what drugs can do to people, that's for sure. I only sell what I'm willing to do. Well, sometimes mushrooms, but, hell, they're organic—just like grass. And I might get coke for someone, but I wouldn't go out of my way to do it—only for long term clients who wouldn't know where else to go. I'm basically a small time operator. Very little risk. Very few middlemen. I've cut way back from the old days, don't even carry over the border myself any more. I'm too old for that shit. Now I meet my supplier in El Paso. And you know what else? I actually declare most of what I make on pot to the tax man. Can you believe that? Those game rooms barely break even, but they're a good cover. No one can say I live beyond my means. I've got that part of my life figured out.

So, you're probably wondering why I'm here. Well, besides the court order, I mean.

Well, it's just a bunch of little stuff, really, but it's beginning to add up—over time, you know. I admit it. Nothing to do with the petty ass little bit of dealing I do. If you can even call it dealing.

Okay, okay, yeah, three things really.

I've thought a lot about what's troubling me and I've scaled it down to just three things. See, didn't I say I liked numbers, was good at math? One. Two. Three. That's probably the main reason I was able to make it in this business and not wind up broke, dead, or in the crapper. I always saved a certain percentage of what I earned. And I never cut anyone short. Not even an eighth of an ounce. Everyone knows I'm fair. Even back in the old days when everyone was enhancing bags with oregano, Ajax, and shit. Well, I can tell you, there's honesty and dishonesty in every profession. Every walk of life has its own set of ethics. You must know that—in your line of work and all.

Sorry. I know I tend to ramble, and if I'm going to cover all three things in an hour . . . Oh? Fifty minutes? I thought it was an hour. Whatever, I better get cooking.

First, my sister, Mary—Mary, Queen of Locks, my grandmother used to call her because she spent so much time on her hair. I can still picture her standing in front of the bathroom mirror, all her equipment—curling iron, blow dryer, rollers, that pink gel—lined up around the edge of the sink. We only had one bathroom and I think she used it more than the rest of us added up.

You see Mary and I were the oldest, just a little over a year apart. Then there's a four year break before Jimmy and Desmond. Mary and I were really close growing up, best friends, even after high school we stayed tight. She was pretty straight, but I know she smoked pot a few times. I even got high with her once. It wasn't till sometime after she got married, maybe it was after her first kid, she started to change, began treating me like I wasn't as good as her. At first, she was just kind of snotty, then she got bitchier and bitchier until it reached this crescendo of out-and-out hate. I didn't do one mean thing to her and she turns on me—even tries to turn our parents against me! Telling them I'm a drug dealer, too dangerous to have around her kids, and all this other crap when she doesn't have the slightest bit of evidence. Can you believe that shit? Her kids were crazy about me. And I was great to them—at least back when she still let me see them. I think she must have been jealous cause I've got my own business and own an apartment house—whatda you think? I mean she doesn't have one shred of evidence that I ever sold drugs. Well, there was one thing, back right before I bought the game rooms, but it wasn't proof or nothing. A judge would have tossed it out of court.

Let me explain, tell you about the final blow-out with her. You won't believe it.

I had been back from Juarez a few days and like always— being the good Irish Catholic boy that I am, heh, heh—I went to visit my parents. After that I stopped over at my sister's house to give her kids the gifts I'd got them: two really cute piñatas, a donkey wearing a sombrero and a . . . there I go again, rambling. You don't need to know all that shit. Anyway, she wasn't home, at the grocery store I think, and her husband let me in. Bob. Big Bob we called him in high school. The kids were really excited to see me. We started wrestling. So, there we were having a great time, rolling around on the living room carpet when in bursts Mary Queen of Locks with steam coming out of her ears and a wad of bills in her hand. She starts screaming, "Get out of my house, you drug dealer, get the hell out!" You see, I had, as we were raised, taken off my boots by her back door, not thinking for a single second that my own sister, no matter how pissed she was at me, would search them! Like I said, I had just got back from Juarez a few days before and I hadn't had a chance to get to my safety deposit box yet, so I had rolled up about ten grand and stuffed it in the toes of my boots. Now, you tell me, what kind of sister would stick her hand into the toes of her brother's boots?

Pretty sick, huh?

She said she saw a corner of a bill sticking out; I don't know, that seems pretty bogus. Next thing I knew she's hitting me, whaling on me, hundred dollar bills are flying, Big Bob, my brother-in-law—he's pretty cool—comes in and pulls Mary off me. I scramble around collecting my dough, the kids are crying, then I'm outta there. Never been in her house since. That's when she really tried to convince my parents I was dealing. That I needed help. But they took up for me. After all, as my dad said, she didn't find drugs in my boots, just cash. And he pointed out that after my grandmother died, they found almost twelve grand under her mattress and she sure as hell wasn't dealing drugs. If it wasn't so sick it would be pretty damn funny—imagining my Granny Fiona dealing, bringing the pot over the border from Juarez. Heh. Heh. Anyway, it's been the silent treatment from my sister since then. Mary Queen of Locks turned into the Ice Queen. She's polite if we both end up at the folks' house at the same time for a holiday or what not, but that's about it.

Okay, okay, one down. Now for story number two. Less of a big deal really. A chick I met last summer, Rosita. Really beautiful. Luscious. Smart, too. Mexican-American. Taught ESL—at least I think that's what she called it, you know, English to foreign kids. Only six years younger than me. Usually I date much younger chicks. I'm not a cradle robber or anything. Just chicks still in their twenties or early thirties. Anyway, Rosita knew right from the start that I sell a little marijuana from time to time. Didn't bother her in the least. She called it a "political act," said she believed marijuana should be legal. Didn't do it much herself, but didn't see a thing wrong with it. She said there were too many Mexicans and black kids behind bars for doing drugs. I mean she was really open-minded, cared about the poor, the down-and-out, and all that bleeding heart shit.

After I had been seeing her about a month, I started really digging her. The funny thing was that I hadn't liked anyone that much in years. I didn't even know I was capable of liking a woman that much, so I decided to open up with her, be totally honest. Women always *say* they want intimacy. Besides, I was even thinking of introducing her to my parents. Never done that before. So, I tell her the truth. That I'm not really from Juarez and my real name is Charles. What do you think she does? Her reaction, I mean. What do you think?

Wow. No wonder you're a shrink, you must be psychic or something.

Yeah, that's exactly what she did. Totally lost it. Blew up, just like Mary Queen of Locks, steam coming out of her ears, the whole bit. Grabs her clothes off the floor, screams a bunch of Spanish swear words at me, then says a bunch of stuff about how I'm "propagating the stereotypical image of Mexicans as drug dealers." How weird is that? Doesn't mind if I sell pot if my name is Carlos but can't take it when I tell her my name is Charles? Freaks out when I try to be honest! After that, she took off and wouldn't return my calls or nothing. Ain't that the strangest thing? You think she might have had a commitment problem or what? I know we're not here to talk about her problems, but I can't help but wonder. Talk about screwed up logic! You'd think she would be happy that I identified with being Mexican American. I mean would a Jew lambaste someone who pretended to be a Jew during the Holocaust? Would a black hate someone who pretended to be black during the fifties in the south?

Yeah, yeah, I know it's not an exact parallel, but I think you must be getting the point. I mean, no wonder I'm a little confused! Okay, so are you ready for number three? It's the weirdest of all. Doesn't make a bit of sense why it even bothers me—another chick, of course—but no one I was close to. I only met her once and that was a few years ago—three, four, five? Who can keep track of time anymore? But she has haunted me ever since. Speaking of time, how much do we have left?

Oh, *okay, okay,* cool, that should be more than enough. By the way, did I tell you I like the way you've decorated your office? Really classy. It's weird. But I can't seem to get my house right—no matter how much money I spend, it still has a kind of cheap look. I guess it needs a woman's touch. Rosita had started to help me a little with the kitchen. She took down my *Nighthawks* poster in the chrome frame (I always dug that over at the AIC, ya know?) and put it in the basement, then hung up these really simple black and white wood cuts in brightly painted frames. Mexican folk art shit. I couldn't believe what a difference they made! Way cooler than I would have guessed. You know it's kind of weird about how I'm bugged by decorating and furniture when that's what I used to use as my cover for years—furniture. I'd rent a U-Haul and pretend like I was moving from Texas to Illinois. I had a hollowed out TV set, a hollowed out couch, a hollowed bed mattress, all lined in metal, and a dresser with a false back. I could move over 300 pounds at a time. I put a bunch of other stuff in the truck too, you know, like boxes of plastic plates and cups, bags of clothing that was ready for the Salvation Army, to make it all look legit. It was so authentic looking that I almost wish I had been pulled over. They would have had to bring out the dogs, and even then I don't know that the dogs would have found it. I won't tell you how I move it now. But believe me, it's foolproof.

Oh, right. Time.

So now—ta-daa!—for the girl behind door number three! Coco, her name was. She must have been eighteen or nineteen, twenty on the far side. She was overweight, real white and wore too much eye make-up, which made her look a little ghostly. Not my type at all. Still, her face was kind of pretty—or would have been if she had lost weight—in a weird way. Knowing and innocent all at once, if that makes any sense. She came over with this kid, Benny, who did a little dealing for me in the high schools. I won't go near those places myself. I deal with a strictly over-eighteen crowd. You know, like they say, no ID, no sale. Heh. Heh. Anyway, they wanted to buy some pot. Another friend was there, maybe a client or two. I don't really remember who, just that we were all on the couch smoking some jays. So there we are sitting around getting high, though I'm not sure she was—like I said, it's a little blurry in my head. Once I hear her name, Coco, it starts to bug me until—bingo—I know where I heard it. A guy I knew 15—maybe even 20, 25—years ago had a kid named Coco. He was a musician, pretty good too, was just on the brink of making the big time when he blew his brains out. It was so unexpected, no one could get over it. He was a friend, but also a client, not a big-time buyer, just a steady supply of pot, mushrooms now and then, nothing heavy. Drugs had nothing to do with his taking the pipe. I mean he wasn't a druggie or anything like that. Just recreational like most of us were back then. I still have a tape of his. He was into some strange sounds—some cool shit. He was a guy I looked up to, Jake, and it turns out that this white lumpy girl in my house is the same Coco, Jake's baby.

Talk about being blown away!

When I realize who she is, I want to connect with her in some way, show her I felt bad about her dad, knew the whole story, so I start talking about him. And I don't know how I said it, but somehow I mention how he did it at home—you know took the bullet in his own garage studio. I know, pretty stupid. A huge error on my part. I admit it. As soon as the words fly out of my mouth, I see it on her face. She didn't know the whole story. She didn't know he had done the deed at home, where apparently this Coco chick and her mom still lived. Oh, she was cool. She pretended she knew. And when I think of it now, I realize that, of course, no one would give all the details about how her old man wasted himself, right in her own back yard! But you see how I can just start rambling and not think before I speak. I did feel bad. I mean really, *really* bad that I had spilled the beans. But that's not what's been haunting me about her for all this time. I was able to get over my being an asshole in a couple of days. It's not like I've never been an asshole before. What I can't get past is the fact that she was in my house at all. Twenty years ago, eighteen, whatever, I'm hanging out with her old man, then it's like no time has passed and I'm hanging out with her, his baby—I remember when she was born—all grown up.

All that gets me thinking. Jake is nothing but a bag of bones, been feeding the worms for years. Once I start thinking about how long Jake has been dead, I start thinking about how all the people I knew back then—except maybe two or three clients—are gone, have moved on. It's like they've all traveled into the future and I'm still here on the couch, getting high with a bunch of punks. It's eerie, like time *itself* has gone on without me. Not that I want to be dead like Jake or living in the burbs with a bunch of rug rats like those other suckers. I like my life. In fact, you must think I'm nuts letting this petty-ass shit bug me when I have the world at my fingertips, except of course this recent brush with the law. Nothing much. Three or five sessions with you and I'm home free. Heh. Heh. But for some damn reason, I can't stop thinking about them—Mary, Rosita, and now this Coco chick. Shit, it's like next thing I know I'll be sitting on the couch and Coco's kids will come waltzing in to buy some pot! Who am I? Some sort of Dorian Gray dealer-dude with a picture up in the attic? I just want to move on, stop thinking about all this crap, clear my head. You must think it's crazy that someone like me would bring up all this petty shit. But I know that if I can just stop those three things from invading my head, I'll be fine. Everything will be like it used to be.

Well, that's it. The whole story. So, what do you think, doc— can you help me?

Storage

Catherine was between homes. That was not to say that she was homeless. For the time being, she lived at Julie's. And, as long as she paid the rent on the storage locker out east in Illinois, she had the makings of a home. Then, in a week, if Catherine was lucky, she would reside in a nice hotel in Australia while she was paid to shoot the bicycle race. She was also between jobs, but that was not unusual in her line of work or even particularly inconvenient. At least in normal circumstances. There were usually only three bills she needed to pay on time: her cell phone, her P.O. box, and the storage locker rent. Now, for pride's sake, she would also have to repay Bjorn the money he had loaned her. Although she could put that off for a while, the thought of him made her realize that she was also between boyfriends.

Rolling over, she groped the floor beside the futon for her watch. When she located it, she held the face close to her eyes. Almost nine. She rarely slept past seven. Too many martinis with Julie last night. If she was going to stop at the bank and post office, then meet Scott for lunch at 11:30, she was going to have to hustle.

Catherine sat up and looked around. What a mess. Julie was a slob. Catherine hated the chaos of sleeping on a collapsing futon in Julie's living room, but Catherine was certainly in no position to complain. Julie's place wouldn't be nearly so crowded if Catherine hadn't stored her belongings—paltry as they were—there while she went to Norway with Bjorn, whom she met while shooting a climb. Catherine had managed to get *National Geographic Traveler* to pay for the flight to Norway and six days while she shot some hikers on the northwest coast. On her way back down the coast, she had taken some great shots of Norwegian surfers. She knew Scott could place them. Surfers in Norway! With cliffs of a fjord rising from the sea in the background. If she was lucky, maybe she could get a cover out of it. Perfect form. Perfect wave. Perfect focus. She also had a bunch of waterfalls that Scott should be able to sell to a stock house. A cover, a few interior shots, and the stock house could bring her well over a thousand dollars. If she got the Australian gig as well, she would be able to get her own place again as soon as she was paid, though the mere thought of apartment hunting agitated her. She probably shouldn't have given up her last place. It was small, nicely located, and relatively inexpensive for Phoenix. But after the first month in Norway, it seemed silly to keep it. She really believed things might work out with Bjorn. She had put Phoenix behind her, not even checking her e-mail until the relationship with Bjorn began to fizzle. When she opened it last week, she found a half dozen missed offers of jobs. And, of course, the e-mail from her brother:

> *Dear Cathy,*
> *Jake's suicide note was found. Please call home as soon as possible.*
> *Love, Danny*

Catherine threw back the duvet, climbed from the futon, and padded barefoot toward the bathroom, careful not to step on any of the objects strewn about. At least Julie had already gone to work. The bathroom was just as messy as the living room. Discarded panties on the floor. Uncapped roll of tooth paste on the back of the toilet. Tubes of lotion and make-up everywhere. Catherine kicked the panties aside and looked in the mirror above the sink. *Shit.* Her face was puffy, eyelids swollen. *Far* too many martinis. She wished, as she had many times before, that she had a servant like Joan Crawford's in *Mommy Dearest* who would supply her with a huge bowl of chipped ice for her face in the morning. Lacking that, she ran the water as cold as she could get it, drenched a washcloth, then pressed it too her face. Ahhhh. *Jake's suicide note was found?*

Who had been looking? It wasn't like he had been a movie star and the tabloids would be after it. Jake was just her oldest brother, no one famous. Besides, where could it possibly have been hiding all these years? And why was it always called a *note*—like it had just been dashed off? Didn't people put thought into the explanations of their suicides? Wouldn't letter be more appropriate? Proclamation? Manifesto?

Catherine repeated the process with the washcloth twice. She began to look human again. She knew she was considered more than merely attractive. She had even modeled for a while. Mostly sportswear—ski jackets and climbing gear. She had a healthy, out-doorsy look. Even now, in her early forties (or, she wondered, was forty-six considered mid?), she continued to easily fit into crowds of young athletes. Most of her friends were a decade younger than she, and she had never had a boyfriend older than herself. Bjorn had been eight years younger. That had been one of the problems, though probably not the biggest. She realized she couldn't live permanently in Oslo and he wouldn't even consider moving to the states.

Please call home as soon as possible?

Where exactly was home? Danny's house, with his wife and two daughters she hadn't seen in years? The state of Illinois? The city of Chicago? Her storage locker? She imagined a phone ringing plaintively in the dark, crammed space.

The more Catherine thought about it, the more it seemed that Danny's brief e-mail reflected how out of touch he was. It had been years since anyone had called her Cathy. She had corrected Danny every time she communicated with him. Cat or Catherine, she didn't care which, just as long as it wasn't Cathy. And another thing, why did she need to get in touch with Danny immediately?

It wasn't as if Jake was waiting for a reply.

After patting her face dry, Catherine applied her foundation and eye make-up. She found it was getting tricky putting on so much make-up, while maintaining a fresh and natural look. The operation seemed to take a minute longer every year. Fortunately, her hair was no problem. She felt blessed in that way. One former boyfriend had called it the color of cream. Neither blonde, white, nor yellow. More like a light beer streaked with half and half. Plus her hair was still thick, worn past her shoulders. All she needed to do was smooth the surface with a heating iron. She never put on lipstick until she was close to her destination. (If re-applied too much, it bled into the tiny cracks beginning to form around her lips.) She wore a natural shade that made her lips the color they were when she was sixteen, an authentic pinkish maroon. Catherine thought of lips the same way her mother talked of made beds. A nicely made bed pulled a whole room together; well-painted lips pulled a face together.

It had been two weeks since Danny had sent the e-mail. She hadn't been to her postal box yet. She imagined there would be a letter from him there too. She had given him her P.O. box number in Phoenix and her e-mail, but not her cell phone. Of course he never bothered to ask her if she had a cell. In his mind, she was still a little girl, incapable of owning a cell phone. How did he think she managed to support herself as a sports and travel photographer with just a P.O. box and checking e-mail on borrowed computers? She was just a little sister to Danny, not someone to be taken seriously or brought into the plans. In fact, she had been a nuisance to both of them, Danny and Jake, not part of their scene. It disgusted her to think how much she used to look up to both of them, particularly Jake. He was nine years older than she; yet she was now fifteen years older than he had been or would ever be.

* * *

Catherine could see Scott from a block away. He waited at the sidewalk café where they usually met, off Central by the art museum, at a little round table in the bright sun, his long legs sticking out from beneath because his knees would hit the underside if he bent them. On the flagstone patio next to him sat an enormous pot of red geraniums. When their eyes connected, she hurried to his table. He rose, offered both cheeks for kisses, and took her portfolio before she sat down. Scott had been her rep since he quit shooting. They had never had a contract and he didn't mind when she got a gig on her own—didn't ask for the usual fifteen percent—but it was generally faster and easier to work through him and pay the percentage.

After they ordered, he leafed through her portfolio. Catherine studied him as he assessed her work. He looked the way she imagined Pinocchio would if he turned into a real boy, grew up, got a tan, and learned to dress stylishly. Scott was tall, slender, and loose-jointed with thick dark-brown hair, cut and parted on the far right, just like Pinocchio's.

He glanced up at her with wide bright eyes, like the glass eyes of a wooden man.

"These are good, Cat, I mean really, *really* good—I can't believe how you just keep getting better . . ."

She tried to look unruffled, but she felt her spine straighten with pride. She knew they were good.

"But a cover, I don't know, Cat, it's been a little slow with the economy and the hits the print media has been taking and a cover, well…"

Her chest deflated. In her mind's eye, she pictured her shoulders slouching, her ribs collapsing.

"Why does there always have to be a 'but'? Can't you ever just say, 'I'll do everything I can to get you a cover'"?

"I *will* do everything I can, you know that. I just don't want to get your hopes up. The market really sucks."

She imagined his nose would grow if he told a lie.

"There you go again, another *but*." She knew she sounded pissed off. She seldom lost her cool. She didn't like to expose emotions and she knew it wasn't his fault. He started to speak again. She held up her hand to silence him. She smiled and tilted her head in what she considered a fetching manner. Scott had—for a short time, long ago—been her lover.

"I'm sorry, I shouldn't have snapped at you, but—now it's my turn for *buts*—I'm kind of desperate. I just went to the bank and mailed some bills and I've got a grand total of four hundred and thirty six dollars left to my name. I spent the last travelers' check before I even left Oslo. If I don't get paid to go to Australia, I'll need to front the money myself to do it on spec. Then when I get back I'll need to move out of Julie's at the same time my storage locker rent is due."

She wished she hadn't mentioned the storage locker. Saying it aloud made her anxious and she knew how Scott felt about the locker. The thought loomed so large in her mind that it just slipped out. The waiter placed their plates in front of them and refilled her iced tea.

"Cat, I'm sorry things didn't work out with Bjorn, but you know that you can't stay out of the scene for three months in these times and expect to plug right back in. When you left, lots of people asked for you specifically. Now most of them who still have gigs have hooked up with other people. That's just the nature of the business."

She smiled again. There was no point making Scott cross with her.

He sighed.

"Don't worry, Cat, I'll get you something, even if it's not a cover. And worst case scenario, I'll front you the money for Australia."

"I'll pay you back."

"I'm not worried."

"You better eat before it gets cold."

Scott hefted his veggie burger while Catherine lifted her fork and approached her salmon salad. At least he would pick up the check and she wouldn't need to feel guilty—it was a business write-off. They ate in the comfortable silence of familiarity. Scott was one of the first people she met when she came to Arizona. He had a degree in journalism and ambitions of becoming a photojournalist, going to war-torn countries to document injustices. At the time they met, he was doing shots for environmental mags while making a little extra money on sports and travel. When it became clear that his dreams weren't going to materialize, that he would never get beyond commercial photography, he gave up and became a rep. On the other hand, Catherine had never wanted to photograph anything but sports and travel, people in motion, particularly athletes. She loved it when she captured the expression on an athlete's face frozen in the peak of action: the contradiction of movement and permanence that occurred in a photograph. Years ago she and Scott used to argue about their choices. He questioned the value of shooting mountain climbers, bicyclists, runners, skiers, couldn't see the point. She could have argued that it was man struggling with nature, with his own mortality, or some such nonsense. Instead she posited that Scott didn't want to do photojournalism for the ultimate good any more than she wanted to do action shots for humanity. She argued that they both did it for the rush. It was just that different things gave them the rush. She still got her rush. He didn't.

"What do you pay for that storage locker these days?"

Her chest tightened. She wished there was a graceful way not to answer, but she had brought the subject up. Best not to dodge the question and make the locker even more of an issue.

"Ninety a month."

Scott whistled. He looked down at his plate and ran a piece of veggie burger through a pool of ketchup.

"I know you don't want to hear this. I'm going to say it anyway. Why don't you get rid of that thing, sell the stuff?" He popped the bite in his mouth. Catherine felt her heart clutch. She pictured the inside of the locker: chairs, headboards, end tables, dressers, linens, bookcases, the old hand-carved chest that her maternal grandmother had brought from Poland, and the dining room table and china cabinet, along with all of her mother's china, carefully wrapped, in boxes. All her mother's possessions. She had particularly loved the china. Her mother was mostly Polish, though there had been a great, great grandmother who was Swedish. Her father was one hundred percent Irish.

"It's all I have."

"You've said yourself, a hundred times, that most of it has no real monetary value."

"It's all that's left of my parents."

"You never even go see it. When was the last time you were in Illinois? Getting rid of the rent on that place would save you over a grand a year, plus whatever an antique dealer would give you for the stuff inside."

"I need it for my future."

Her tone forced him to switch subjects. Or maybe it was the word "future." They were the oldest in their immediate circle of friends. The only two over forty. They had stopped talking about the future around the same time they had stopped arguing about the value of their work.

* * *

Catherine spent the entire afternoon at the gym. Her own membership had lapsed, so Julie gave her a guest pass. Getting her endorphins going usually cleared Catherine's head and reduced her depression. But the whole time on the elliptical, she couldn't banish images of her mother's china. The yellow finch on a branch floating in the center of each plate. Delicate tea cups with yellow rims and matching saucers. Catherine's father had died while she was in high school, her mother during her second year of college. The small amount of cash they had saved—$18,000—was given to Danny. He had used some of it to help pay for Catherine to do a third year of college. The rest of the possessions were divided less fairly: Jake got the house, Danny the car, and Catherine the furnishings. The only thing of any real value was the house, a brick bungalow on the near northwest side of Chicago. Catherine understood there was a perverse logic to her parents' apportionment. They figured that as the oldest son, Jake deserved the castle; Danny, the son who was still single at the time, should get the car; and the girl would want the furnishings, a dowry of sorts. She didn't blame her parents. Her brothers should have known better. They should have offered to pool everything, sell it, and divide the proceeds. Not only didn't they offer—they wouldn't even listen to her suggestions. She hated the fact that she had once idolized her brothers.

Before Jake moved into the house, Catherine had a yard sale of everything detachable, all the appliances—the washer and dryer, the television, the mixer, even the stove and refrigerator. She sold the old Venetian blinds for a quarter a window. Then she had everything else moved to a storage locker just outside of the city. With the money from the yard sale, she headed west. First to San

Francisco, then Montana, and finally moving permanently to Arizona. She imagined she would be back for the furnishings in a year or two, when she got a big enough place. In fact, in the last twenty years, she had only visited the locker four times, the same number of times over the years that she had visited Danny and his family. He had also been west a few times on business. She was angry with him for siding with Jake—though she realized he was almost as big a loser financially in the deal as she and had acted generously toward her. She'd never spoken to Jake again, didn't even return for his funeral, though she did visit his grave the few times she visited her parents' graves.

* * *

A note on the counter said that Julie had gone to Sedona for the night. Next to the note sat a half full bottle of Shiraz and a large flat pizza carton with two pieces left. Couldn't Julie have taken the time to re-cork the bottle and put the pizza in the fridge? For a moment at the gym, Catherine considered asking Julie if they could share the place. She imagined buying a pretty Japanese screen to divide off a section of the living room for herself. If she unpacked her boxes and helped Julie get organized, there would be plenty of room. And as an official roommate, Catherine would be able to put her foot down about guests. The mess on the counter changed her mind. As much as she loved Julie, they were simply not compatible. Besides, Catherine was probably too old for a roommate. She hadn't had one in years.

Catherine rinsed out a glass and poured herself some of the Shiraz. Not bad, at least it had been given enough time to breathe. She sat on a counter stool and drank the wine as she decided how to spend her evening. Many of her friends didn't even know she was back in town. Someone would be free for dinner or a drink, or would gladly cancel other plans in order to catch up with her. The problem was that she didn't feel like going through the whole story of Bjorn and how their relationship unraveled. Furthermore, she shouldn't be spending any money. She might as well just stay in, take a long bath, maybe give herself a facial. She had just lugged all her photo equipment half way across the world. She needed a break before she faced everyone.

At least she had the apartment to herself. She finished the glass and poured what was left of the bottle. Her stomach felt a little raw so as she drank she nibbled the pointed tip of a piece of the pizza. Thai chicken pizza. The unusual taste actually exploded in her mouth. She took a larger bite, quickly chewed and swallowed. It tasted wonderful. All she had eaten was the salmon salad and iced tea. No breakfast. No coffee. No bread. She didn't plan to eat the entire piece, but ended up eating both pieces, quickly gobbling. Immediately afterwards, she was depressed. Her whole afternoon in the gym undone in a matter of fifteen minutes. Not to mention that the cheese would probably make her break out. So unfair to be getting wrinkles and still having to worry about pimples if she wasn't careful.

To make herself feel better, she tidied the apartment a little before running her bath. The hot water softened her tense muscles. Whenever the water began to cool, she ran more hot by twisting the faucet handle with her toes.

She luxuriated in the tub until the wine had worn off and the hot water had run out. By the time she was dried and in her nightgown, it was only seven p.m. The evening spread out before her like exposed film that could never be shot or processed. Wasted before it was even used. And the wine was gone. She searched the cupboards until she found a sealed bottle of Jack Daniels on a top shelf. Usually she drank wine at home or martinis for nights out. She only liked white liquor—vodka or gin. But this would have to do. She remembered her brothers had liked bourbon. Danny drank it when he took her out to dinner on one of his business trips. She remembered seeing Jake with a bottle of Jack once. He was standing in the living room with Danny, holding the bottle by the throat. She couldn't recall any of the circumstances surrounding the image. Only his hand clasping the bottle neck.

Catherine twisted the cap, ripping the seal, located a single tray of ice in the freezer, and tried to think of something to do while she drank. Turning on the television would depress her and she couldn't call anyone without going through her whole tale of woe. Next to the futon was the murder mystery she had planned to read on the flight over but had never taken out of her carry-on. She filled a glass with ice and settled into a corner of the couch next to her futon. She poured a glass, keeping the bottle on the table beside her. A martini would have been better. She loved the way the flat surface of a martini, level with the brim of the glass, reminded her of icy mountain lakes. But she would have to do with the mild crackle of ice as she poured her first glass of bourbon. Catherine might as well enjoy it because even if she only drank a glass, she would need to buy Julie a whole new bottle to make up for breaking the seal.

Catherine swallowed, the liquid burning her throat, and opened the paperback, cracking the spine so it would be easy to hold spread apart. She read the first line: *When he saw the position of the body, Detective Marsh knew it couldn't have been a suicide.* Suicide. She put the book down, open on her lap. Was the universe conspiring against her?

It was amazing how often the subject of suicide came up. In this very room, at a party two summers ago, someone had started a game that entailed asking people how they would kill themselves if need be. Everyone had an answer, as if they had seriously thought about the question. Most of the women said pills or slit wrists. The guys favored driving off cliffs. Catherine was the only one who had refused to go along.

"I wouldn't do it."

"What if your entire life was falling apart?"

"I'd move. I'd go somewhere else, start a new life."

"What if you were broke?"

"I'd panhandle and hitchhike."

"What if you couldn't walk and you were sick and had nothing to lose."

"This game is ridiculous. Suicide is a selfish act; I wouldn't do it."

"What if it was to save someone you loved, how would you do it then?"

She hadn't told any of her Arizona friends except Scott (who wasn't there that night) about Jake's suicide, so she couldn't really blame them for insensitivity, only immaturity. Not that one had to be immature to mention suicide. It was astonishing how quick people were to say "I'm going to kill myself" at the slightest problem. The first time she got a photograph in *Sports*, she was bothered by the way they cropped it and wrote a long letter explaining the error to the photo editor. When she showed the draft to Scott, he called it the longest professional suicide note he had ever read. She didn't send it.

Catherine finished her drink, returned to the kitchen for the last of the ice. Sitting perfectly still on the couch, she sipped her bourbon, the book back in her lap, as the night took shape around her. The table lamp seemed to become brighter as the darkness thickened. She thought of her family, an indulgence she only allowed herself infrequently. She couldn't help the many times daily they flashed into her mind. But she could usually prevent herself from dwelling on them.

All her friends knew about her past was that her parents were dead and she had two older brothers out east. No one knew that one of the brothers resided in a grave. She didn't contribute much to conversations about siblings—just "my brothers were much older so I didn't know them well. I was an accident." When she first heard about Jake's death, that was the first word to pop into her head— accident. Then, when the word suicide came up, she thought it had to be a mistake, a gun-cleaning incident gone wrong or a murder made to look like a suicide. Before the inheritance issue, Jake had been her hero. Danny had been close enough in age to Catherine to seem like an older buddy; Jake had moved away from home when she was still in grade school. Danny was pale and Irish-looking like their father; Jake was tanned, with creamy hair like her own. She remembered his "hippie" phase best, when he wore his hair just past his shoulders. Thick vanilla fringe. Leather vests. He looked like a Viking, forging into worlds outside the home that she could never enter. When he shot himself, the age gap seemed a blessing. She never blamed his suicide on their falling out. She knew she wasn't important enough to him to cause such an act. Now, as she poured a third glass of bourbon, she couldn't help but wonder. Surely it didn't help to have his worshipful little sister completely cut him off. Maybe her scorn added to a series of other causes. Did he mention her at all in the note?

Catherine doubted it.

She took a long swallow. Her veins burned. She felt a flush in her cheeks.

Jake had a daughter. Just a little kid at the time of his death, she would be in her twenties now. Catherine wondered what had become of her. Did Jake's widow still live in Catherine's parents' house? She had made a point of never asking Danny about them. Danny sent Christmas photos of his own daughters, but Catherine hadn't seen Jake's little girl since she was a baby. It was weird to think she had a niece out there somewhere whom she didn't even know. Maybe this was the time to make contact? The note provided an excuse.

When she thought about it, Catherine had to admit that she was curious. Why would someone so beautiful and talented take his own life? He was a musician. "On the verge of fame" was the expression most often associated with him. Actually, she might have only heard it once or twice, but that was the way it was with things one heard or did as a child—they multiplied with age. Perhaps he wasn't even as handsome as she remembered, though his was the face that usually came to her in a moment of triumph: when she captured an astonishingly good image, made a big sale, beat out another photographer for a sought-after gig, or won an award. He was the person she wanted to tell. She remembered running to him with a drawing or a school paper when he visited her parents' home, playing the flute for him on the rare occasions when she could get him to sit and listen. He was a real musician; what he said meant more than what her school orchestra leader said. She pictured his fingers on the strings of his guitar, unusually long and well-manicured for a man. His face, golden and broad, with high cheekbones sharp enough for birds to perch, shocking blue eyes, and his thick mane of hair. His face appeared full force in her mind's eye.

Oh, my God, she realized, *Jake looked like Bjorn. Shit.*

Fury and confusion welled in her throat, acid rising. She threw her paperback across the room. It slammed against a bookshelf. Her hand trembled.

No, she told herself, *I'm just drunk, imagining things.*

She finished her glass. Is it possible she hadn't noticed such a likeness until now? Placing the empty glass on the side table, she stood, rising a little too quickly. She veered forward and stumbled, whacking her shin on the coffee table.

Yikes!

Shrieking, Catherine folded the injured leg to her chest and hopped around the room. Her voice rose in little shouts. *Ouch. Ouch. Ouch.* When the pain started to subside, she laughed, glad there was no one to witness her drunken foolishness. She kneeled in front of the futon to retrieve her knapsack from beneath it. A flurry of dust balls collected as she stretched out on her belly and grabbed. She wanted the pack of photos in the sack. She had taken them at one of the largest Norwegian waterfalls. After using up all her own film on professional shots, she had had to buy a disposable camera in order to take photos of Bjorn. The knapsack was all the way at the far wall. She pushed with her toes, extending her right arm, until she was able to reach a strap.

The photos were still in the saffron-colored processing envelope. Catherine kneeled back to shuffle through them. *Yes, yes, there was definitely a resemblance.* In fact the more she looked, the more she couldn't see *any* difference between Jake and Bjorn. The problem was that she didn't have a photo of Jake to compare. All the family albums were in the storage locker in Illinois.

Tossing the photos on the coffee table, Catherine slid back, pulled herself up onto the couch, and threw her head back. She stretched out the injured leg so she could massage her shin. She poured another glass of bourbon. Most of the ice had melted, but oddly, the liquor didn't taste as strong now.

The last time she had seen Jake was on the day of her garage sale. She had posted signs all over the neighborhood and lined the garage in the back alley with everything from the house that she wasn't putting in storage. Though Jake hadn't moved in, he came for the sale, offering to help, teasing her, making wisecracks, a big grin on his face.

"Oh, you're taking the blinds? Well, I suppose that technically they're not part of the house, but it's going to get awful bright without anything on the windows."

He acted like she was a little girl setting up a lemonade stand. She ignored him, pretended he wasn't there. He didn't bother to stay the whole time. He needed some reaction from her to keep his attention. It was the last time she ever saw him.

She had another drink.

Desultorily, she wondered if people sent suicide e-mails these days. If so, they would be able to get everyone they knew in one swoop. Of course, if they did send to their entire address book, they would need to be quick on the trigger. One never knew who might be logged on, even at three in the morning, and come to the rescue.

"Jake?" she said aloud, her voice plaintive in the empty room. She drained her glass. "What were you thinking?"

Since she was out of ice, Catherine didn't bother to pour another glass. She drank straight from the bottle, something she had never done before with hard liquor. It felt liberating, provocative, and she liked the way her lips circled the opening—the way she imagined her older, cool brothers probably drank when they were young. Dust balls clung to her nightgown and a lump was forming on her shin. So much for the bath and a quiet night at home.

"Jake, if you can hear me, give me a sign."

She hiccupped, and then laughed at her own stereotypical drunken behavior.

She wondered if Danny would think Bjorn looked like Jake. The thought led to another one that she hadn't had in a long time. *Maybe I should go to Chicago, have a real visit with Danny and his family, look up Jake's daughter in person.* Given that Chicago was a hub, it might even be cheaper to fly either to or back from Australia via Chicago. She began feeling sorry for herself. She was broke and alone. Who else was there to turn to but her only living brother? Wasn't that what people did when they hit bottom? Maybe she should give some of the photo albums to Jake's daughter or Danny's girls. Regardless of whether she was justified in her anger toward Jake, she had no right to hold a grudge against the girls or Danny. He didn't support her in her fight with Jake, but he had helped her with college and once offered to help her with a down payment for a house. Her reply had been flippant. Too little too late. Was it really too late? She had to admit that there was a possibility she had been unfair to him. After all, he hadn't inherited the house. The car probably had less inherent value than the furnishings. *Tomorrow*, she decided, *I will call him. Tomorrow.* She could spend an entire week in Chicago, take him or his daughters or maybe Jake's girl out to the storage locker to help decide what, besides the albums, was worth keeping.

Tilting back her head, she took a long swallow.

Why *had* she kept the locker all these years? Except for her camera equipment, she traveled lightly. People always marveled at her minimalist approach to life. Her apartments were also spare. She didn't see them that way; she always envisioned how they would look once all her parents' belongings were moved in. Her mother's yellow finch china. The hand-carved chest from Poland. The piles of photo albums. Catherine wasn't making space in her apartments, she was saving it. As long as she had the locker, she didn't notice what she didn't have in her possession.

Not that Catherine had stored everything. She had been careful about what she kept in the locker, throwing out most of her old toys. Strangely, she had kept her old tin dollhouse. She pictured it sitting on top of the china cabinet in the storage space. When she was a little girl she had wanted her father to buy or build her a real wooden dollhouse; instead they had given her the tin one. Open in the back, the house was divided with tin walls into six rooms. The downstairs included a living room, kitchen, and front hall with stairs that walked into the ceiling. Upstairs were two bedrooms— one for the parents and one for a baby—and a bathroom. All the details were printed on the walls, inside and out: curtains, shutters, a rose lattice, front steps. The downstairs windows didn't open, and the upstairs ones were cut permanently open with sharp tin edges. She had had to fly her doll family between floors since there was no actual opening above the stairs for her to walk them through the ceiling to the second floor. At the time she had desperately wanted a more authentic house with moving pieces. Real miniature pictures hanging on the walls. Real little rugs instead of printed ones.

Now she longed for the tin house.

Next to the china cabinet was Jake's first guitar, a battered, old hand-me-down. She had smuggled it out of the house without telling him.

"Jake," she said again, this time just a whisper.

Whenever she pictured Jake's suicide, it was as if he was caught by a camera mid-act, right as the bullet entered his skull, drops of blood perpetually poised mid-air, red petals sprouting from the wound. His teeth tight in a grimace. In her mind, he was arrested forever in the netherworld between life and death. The tiny window between action and non-action.

If she ever did kill herself, Catherine thought she would make it look like an accident, a tumble from a cliff during a shoot.

She felt her eyes well up.

Damn, I am drunk, even drunker than the night before. Tears slipped out. Shit. She started to cry, tears streaming down her hot cheeks. She felt her shoulders heave. Sob. She was sobbing. Shaking. *Oh, my God*, she thought, *how long has it been since I've cried?* Not once during the break-up with Bjorn. Not at Jake's death. Now her whole body shook. She felt violent retching in her ribs. In her chest. Waves racked all her limbs. The weeping lasted for a solid ten minutes, rising and falling in intensity. Then, she wiped her eyes and laughed. She hoped she wasn't becoming a sentimental drunk. Their father had always cried when he drank too much. Fortunately that hadn't been too often. Catherine started to stand but felt too dizzy and sank back on the couch.

She knew the news from Scott wasn't going to be good. He might even be less aggressive in pushing her work in order to teach her a lesson about being gone too long. Scott was not beyond behaving punitively at times. She hadn't considered it before, but now she wondered if he might be jealous of her spontaneity, her growing talent?

She took a hard swallow. Less than a sixth of the bottle was left. So much bourbon. She remembered her mother talking about "gin blossoms," little roses of broken blood vessels that sprouted on the noses and cheeks of gin drinkers. It was probably good that all Julie had in the house was bourbon. *No point in stopping now.* Catherine guzzled the remainder of the bottle, savoring the burn in her throat. She licked the bottle's glass lips.

* * *

The bell signal to start the race didn't stop, even after the runners took off. The loud ringing hurt her head. Why didn't anyone notice? She couldn't concentrate on framing her shot. This was the Olympics; she didn't want to blow it. Why didn't they cut the noise? Then she realized it was the phone. She wasn't at the Olympics. She was plastered on Julie's couch, her cell phone on the coffee table pealing. Catherine started to sit but a sharp pain stabbed her behind the eyes, so instead she simply reached for the phone without moving from her back. It was Scott. He didn't even say hello.

"Cat, you're not going to believe this."

"Let me guess, no cover?" Her tongue felt thick, her mouth dry.

"No, not a cover, *two covers!*"

"What?" Despite the pounding in her head, she pulled herself up.

"*Surfer* took one for the cover and six of the surfers for the inside, and then—talk about luck—I get an e-mail calling for shots of Norway. It turns out that *Around the World* is doing a special feature on Norway. They took a waterfall for the cover and ten of the others! And that's not all. I got you five days in Australia, completely covered."

She could barely breathe. This was the most money she had ever earned at one time. Two covers. She could rent a place as soon as she returned from Australia. She could repay Bjorn. And, she realized with more relief than she would have anticipated, she could pay the next six months on the locker.

Catherine laughed when she hung up and noticed her nightgown. It was filthy! She glanced at the photos on the coffee table. What had she been thinking? Bjorn didn't resemble Jake in the slightest. She had just been drunk. Way too drunk. She wouldn't do that again.

Her head hammered, her throat burned, and her eyelids were swollen half shut from crying the night before. When she stood up, her shin throbbed. She hobbled to Julie's computer, all her muscles aching, and typed in Danny's e-mail address:

Dear Danny,
Thanks for keeping me informed on current developments regarding Jake's suicide, but I have no interest in his note. That's all in my past and I never think about the past. I hope your family is well. Catherine

She tapped SEND without even re-reading her message. How could she have even considered dismantling the locker? She didn't have her own house, a boyfriend, a husband, a permanent job. Without the contents of the storage locker—the furniture of her childhood, the makings of her parents' marriage, the chairs her brothers had sat on for every meal of their boyhood—she would be left with nothing to lose.

How We Move the Air

Coco reclined in the corpse position, *Shavasana*, the final pose of her prenatal yoga class, and tried, as her instructor quietly urged, to let her mind go blank.

"Picture a white light moving with your breath, streaming through your body, gently massaging the aches and pains. Think of nothing except the soft white light and its healing power, its peacefulness."

The instructor's voice was low, monotone, and soothing. Yet the only white light Coco's mind could produce was glaring, more like the interrogation lights used by the detectives in the *noir* films that she and Andrew liked to rent. Contrary to feeling peace, Coco's interior felt electrified. She couldn't dim the light. And her mind jumped from one thought to another. She hadn't been able to focus on anything since her uncle had e-mailed her two days earlier. She had been sitting at the computer when his e-mail arrived. The address, *ddoyle@yahoo*, had materialized before her eyes like a sunken object floating to the surface of a pond. Why did her uncle want to meet her? After so many years? What would he say? What would she say?

"Now, gather the white light in your belly and caress the form growing within," commanded the instructor.

In disobedience, Coco kept her white light at bay. It might be dangerous to force the intense brightness onto her baby. Coco imagined the fetus's tightly clenched eyelids bursting open in shock. The image produced an involuntary giggle, which she quickly suppressed.

"Now, when you are ready, *but only when you are ready*"—how did the instructor manage to maintain a monotone while stressing certain phrases?—"roll to the right side and stay in the fetal position for a moment."

Holding her huge belly to ease the turn, Coco flopped to her right. A fetal within a fetal, she thought, a room full of swirls spiraling deeper inward, making the floor resemble a giant tray of cinnamon muffins. She was probably the most pregnant of any of the women in the class.

"Slowly, begin to rise, one vertebra at a time, into a sitting position. Do so only when you are completely ready. Remember, the corpse position is the most important position of your practice today. *Shavasana* prepares us for a peaceful death."

Coco wondered, fleetingly, if it was appropriate to talk of death in a prenatal yoga class. The thought led her to her father, which made her wonder if he would have died less violently if he had practiced yoga. She hadn't thought much of her father's death in the last few years since she met Andrew. Talking to Andrew almost seemed to cure her obsession. But how could she not think of her father when she would be meeting his brother in fewer than thirty minutes? It was as impossible as staying focused and imagining a soft white light. Coco just wanted to get through the Ohms, pull her sweat clothes on over her t-shirt and shorts, and securely tie her shoes. The thick snow flurries had been unexpected, and she worried about walking the slippery three blocks to the diner, the Daily Bar and Grill, at the corner of Lincoln and Wilson, where she was to meet her uncle.

* * *

The overcast sky and the great gusts of wind and snow made the time seem more like 4 p.m. than noon. Large flakes collected in Coco's eyelashes. She blinked and concentrated on watching her feet. She didn't want to fall at this stage in her pregnancy and bring on premature contractions. Under the fresh three inches, patches of ice were invisible. And bracing against the wind was difficult. The biting current ate right through her sweat pants, almost as if she were walking along bare-legged in the blizzard. Giddy with nerves and anticipation, she giggled aloud at the image of her naked legs, then immediately sobered. What if her uncle could see her approaching? Her appearance was bad enough without manically laughing to herself. Frozen wisps of hair spun around her face, and her jacket barely buttoned over her belly. Plus her hands were pink and chapped.

She had lost her gloves two days before. She wished she had taken more time to prepare for this meeting. Why hadn't she just skipped yoga this morning? She should have dressed better and gone straight from home to the diner, so that she could have been waiting in a booth with her hair brushed and a touch of lipstick, watching for him—instead of the other way around.

Grasping the door handle for balance, Coco climbed the two steps into the anteroom of the Daily Bar and Grill, caught her breath, and opened the door into the dining area. As she adjusted to the darkness, she saw that only a few people had braved the weather to eat lunch out. In a booth in the back a man sat alone, his face under-lit from the little shaded lamp attached to the wall. He looked too old. Coco knew her uncle would be in his fifties, yet she hadn't expected him to look old. She must have been staring because he smiled and waved in welcome.

By the time she had walked the ten feet to the booth, her coat smelled of damp wool. Melting snow already dripped from Coco's coat in the overheated room. And her hair had started to thaw.

"Hello, I'm Danny," said the man, rising as far as the booth would allow without making a complete exit.

"I'm pregnant," she said, immediately regretting opening with a non-sequitur. But she hadn't wanted him to think that she was just fat. In fact, at eight months, she was still a few pounds lighter than her top high school weight. Danny's eyes dropped to her belly. He smiled and slid out of the booth to help her off with her coat.

"Well, then, I guess I'm Great Uncle Danny."

"How were the roads? Slippery?" she asked.

"I can't believe it," he said, seeming—fortunately, she felt—not to hear her banal question. "I'm a great uncle, and Jake would be a grandfather if he were alive."

He shook his head in disbelief.

"Jake, *a grandfather.*"

"I'm taking yoga and eating really well, prenatal yoga. Healthy food. Andrew wants me to have the baby at home." Why was she prattling on so inanely? She had as little control over her words now as she had had over her thoughts twenty minutes earlier in class. She told herself to calm down, that there would be time to tell her uncle about Andrew and her life later, yet she couldn't stop. As she eased herself into the booth, she continued chattering. "Andrew, that's my husband, only his parents call him Andy, he prefers Andrew. He likes things all natural, organic food for instance, at least now he does, but says it's my choice, of course. I'm all for natural, but no drugs in the hospital, I'm not sure. My mom's a nurse, so she thinks . . ."

"Yolunda? You look like both her and Jake." Danny squinted as if to see beyond her skin, the way Roy, her former boyfriend, the self-proclaimed psychic, had before he saw a vision. "Yes, I see Jake in you, too. It looks like a transparency of Yolunda's face has been put on top of Jake's."

Coco tried to see her father in Danny, at least the photo-graphic memories she had of her father. She had been too young when he died to remember him more than dimly, a few random images of him. His strong young hands reaching for her. The long fingers. His thick, buttery, longish hair brushing her cheek. Danny was a middle-aged man, with thinning, blondish red hair and a jaw-line that was beginning to fall. Her father had never grown old. He would forever be a young musician. That was the good thing about his suicide, remaining forever young. Coco squirmed, afraid of what she might say. She was thankful when the waitress interrupted to take their orders.

Danny ordered a burger, which came in a red plastic basket with fries. Coco had soup, warming her hands on the curved sides of the bowl before lifting her spoon. She sipped slowly in order to calm her nerves. She remembered what Andrew had said before she left that morning. *He'll be as nervous as you. This is just as weird for him. Besides, he's the one who should feel bad. He was the grown-up. He should have gotten in touch with you before now.* She hadn't thought about her father's family's responsibility to her and her mom when she was growing up. The hole created by her father's absence eclipsed all other absences.

"So, why didn't you get in touch with us before now?" she asked.

"I did, well, just a few times in the beginning, but your mom, well she didn't seem that open to it, I guess."

"Oh, yeah, Mom can be like that—or could be. She's getting better, more open. I think she's excited about the baby."

"Well, still, that's not an excuse—I mean on my part—not your mother's. But the whole thing was so painful and I was starting my own family back then. But time, well, you can't know it until it happens, time has a way of advancing faster than you expect, and then suddenly circling back," he said, looking a bit startled that such a remark had emerged from his mouth. Was it because of the state-ment's intimacy or its poetic nature? "It's hard to explain to someone your age. But ten years ago, Jake seemed like a brother in a former life. Now, well, now I wouldn't be shocked if he were to walk through that door."

He lifted his huge burger for a bite, chewed thoughtfully, and looked past Coco, as if he were imagining Jake entering the room.

"I think I know what you mean," said Coco. She thought of how thoroughly she had managed to erase her first real lover, Roy, from her thoughts, and the power with which he had reentered her consciousness during her last year at college in DeKalb. It took only minutes to locate an article about him on the internet. He was incarcerated in Statesville in Joliet. It turned out he had never paid a dime of taxes for his psychic business. And when caught, he had attacked one of the policemen. Coco wrote him, and he put her on his visitor's list. She wanted to talk to him, get a sense of whether he had any remorse. This time, her roommate, Vicky, drove her there to visit him, the weekend of graduation. They laughed when they approached the main entrance. Except for the barbed wire curling along the perimeters, the prison looked like a college. STATESVILLE was spelled out in colored petunias in the front. Vicky waited in the car. Inside, the place seemed more like a prison than the exterior had indicated, particularly when they patted Coco down and searched her purse.

"So, why now?" Coco persisted with her uncle.

"I have something for you," he said.

"I have something for you too," she said, and reached into her pocket for the envelope. Until this moment she hadn't been sure she would give it to him but had brought it in case he turned out to be someone she liked. The paper felt soggy; snow must have blown inside her pocket. Coco slid the card across the table. "It's an invitation to my baby shower. It's in two weeks. Andrew is superstitious. He didn't want a shower until we were almost there. It's sort of weird, because he's a scientist, at least he's going to be. He's doing his post doc. Mom will be there. I know you don't really know me, and you don't have to bring a present . . ."

Her voice faded on the last words. Danny was sinking back in his seat in what seemed like embarrassment or, maybe, sadness; Coco didn't know him well enough to be sure. She looked at her invitation still sitting in the center of the table, between his basket and her bowl. Her carefully written script, *Mr. and Mrs. D. Doyle*, was smeared across the front of the envelope.

"Don't feel you have to come, I mean I know it's kind of weird, but we don't have much family and so I just thought . . ."

"No, no, it's not that. I'd be honored to come. It's just that I didn't know you were pregnant and now I'm not so sure I should give you what I brought for you. It's not as nice as what you're giving me. In fact, not nice at all. I don't want to upset you."

"What is it?"

"A letter, from your father . . ."—ice seemed to sear up Coco's spine—"I've had it for a few years. It was addressed to me but I didn't actually receive it until . . . um, it was sent to me a few years ago. At the time I thought about sending it to you, and then, well, you know what I said about time. It got away from me. Now, well, my youngest daughter just went off to college, so my wife and I are moving to a smaller place, and I came across the letter in my desk. I couldn't throw it away, but I don't want it anymore. He wrote it right before he died. If you want, I can keep it until a more appropriate time."

"No," she said, her voice firm for the first time that day. "Now is a good time. I want the letter now."

* * *

Andrew was waiting for her. The second she walked in the door, he put on a kettle of water to boil for tea.

"So, what happened? What did he want?"

Coco hoisted herself onto one of the two matching bar stools they kept at the tall, butcher block table in the center of the room. The stools and the table were their few items of furniture that hadn't been acquired at a garage sale or a second hand store. She pulled the letter out of the waistband of her sweatpants, where she had slid it to keep dry on her way home. She placed it on the table.

"My father's suicide note."

Andrew pulled the other stool directly across from her and climbed onto it.

"That *fucker*, that dumb jerk, couldn't he see that you were pregnant?"

"No, no, it wasn't like that. He was nice. He didn't want to give it to me after he realized I was pregnant. I insisted."

"Have you read it?"

"No, not yet."

Andrew stared at her, waiting. He was a patient person. He could wait. Coco loved that about him. She also loved that he loved her, that he was outraged at her pain. But she didn't want him to feel any pain on her account. When he was upset or cold the thin red scars on his face—emanating from his mouth like three cat whiskers on either side—grew darker, a fierce maroon. In high school, Andrew had been a cutter, slashing up his arms and legs. He had worn long pants and sleeves to cover up. His parents hadn't noticed until he sliced his face with a razor blade. Deep, thin cuts, more carefully and ritualistically drawn than those on his arms. Then, they put him in a hospital. That was one of the reasons he hated hospitals, why he wanted to have the baby at home. The other was that he worked in a hospital now, doing research on brain disorders. He said that hospitals were fine places to work, but dangerous for people who were sick. Coco's mother, who worked in a different hospital across town, disagreed.

The teakettle whistled, and Andrew rose to make them both a cup of chamomile.

Coco had met Andrew when he was a grad student involved in a study of the connections between suicide, creativity, and bipolar disorders. At the time, she had just moved back from DeKalb to Chicago to go to grad school herself, to study book and paper arts. She was a perfect subject for the research, the daughter of a suicide, studying art herself. She told herself that she participated because the money was good and the work easy—filling out forms and answering questions. She hadn't expected to learn anything real about her father. Nor had she expected to fall in love.

Andrew told her about his scars, how he had been back before they met, and she felt an immediate bond. She thought of them as two survivors. When Andrew placed her mug on the table, Coco spoke.

"I think it's good that I read his letter now, put it behind me before the baby is born."

"I thought it was behind you. You know your father undoubtedly suffered from bipolar disorder; *he* didn't know that, so whatever he says in the letter is suspect. It's what he *thinks*, not what really happened."

"His version still means something," said Coco. She felt her voice rising. "People aren't just chemistry sets walking around on two legs, waiting for their genetic predispositions to kick in. Now, please, can I have some time to read it by myself?"

Leaving his mug behind, Andrew sulked out of the kitchen. As quickly as she had become annoyed with him, Coco was sorry to have raised her voice and hurt his feelings. Andrew was right to remind her of what she had learned from the study. Though incomplete—because she wasn't able to get enough information from her mother—the retroactive diagnosis suggested her father had suffered from great mood swings. During the manic highs, he had been incredibly creative, composing continually. During the lows, he didn't seem to do anything except lie around and get high. The results were consistent with the findings in Andrew's field of research and other studies. Artists suffered from extreme manic fluctuations more frequently than the average population, and, therefore, killed themselves more frequently. To Andrew, her father's suicide was nearly that simple.

Coco opened the letter and read. There was a moment of exhilaration at seeing her father's handwriting for the first time, followed moments later by disappointment. The letter consisted of pages of delusional writing. The content taught her little of interest—besides the fact that her father seemed to have been cheating on her mother—until the last line: *It's the only way to move the air.* She sat up straighter and read the letter again, every crazy page.

"Andrew!" she called. "Come here."

"Yeah?" he said, sliding into the kitchen on his socks. Without his scars and his goofy behavior, he would be traditionally handsome. Coco was glad for both of these imperfections.

"Listen to this," she said and began to read aloud:

> *I feel like I weigh a thousand pounds. I'm down so far that I can barely get off the mattress. I'm sinking so deep that soon I'll disappear & become a part of the fucking fabric. I haven't written a thing since that shitty rejection. Nor made any sounds. Sound. It's all in how we move the air. . .and that's over for me . . . .*

"That's typical," said Andrew. "In the low period the bipolar individual is rarely productive, and the lack of production exacerbates . . ."

"No, quiet, let me finish."

> *THIS piece could change it all, open me up again, and revolutionize the concept of eliminating intention when composing. It's the only way to move the air.*

She looked up at Andrew, trembling with dread and anticipation.

"What?" he asked.

"Don't you get it? The gunshot was some sort of work of art. The sound! He was creating some sort of soundscape. You know he was into all that audio art stuff, the randomness of sounds rather than formal music. I'm not even sure he planned to kill himself. Maybe it was just about random shots in a room. I mean he does say he wanted to eliminate intention. All that John Cage shit he was into."

"Coco, I don't know, I know that you don't want me to categorize him but it's not unusual when a bipolar artist feels played out." Andrew frowned before continuing. "Remember Schumann, the classic example of a composer. Besides, if it was some type of weird composition why didn't he record it?"

"Maybe it was performance art?"

"Performance for whom?"

Coco's shoulders sank.

"Maybe you're right."

"Maybe I'm wrong," said Andrew. "Even if I'm right, you still know that his death didn't have anything to do with you. It has to do with depression, and, now, *maybe* with moving air, which seems to be about not being able to make music, but not you, not because he didn't care about you."

"Yeah, I guess," said Coco.

Andrew took the letter from her, folded it, and placed it under the bowl of fruit and unpaid bills in the center of the butcher block. Gently, he wrapped his arms around her head and pulled it to his chest.

"Now, you've read it. Let's put it behind us."

* * *

No matter how hard she tried, Coco couldn't put the letter behind her. So, at the end of her pregnancy, when she should have been envisioning soft white lights and nesting, Roy and her father had taken up residence in her consciousness. Her father, because of the letter. Roy, because of the link to her father, both as a twisted father figure himself and through his link to the spirit world, his telepathic connections. Her father had named her Coco after a blues singer he had admired at one time. Roy had improvised by calling her Coco Bean. And now, Roy was the one person who could make contact with her father. She couldn't talk to Andrew about any of this since he didn't believe in clairvoyance or the spirit world. And though he had never met Roy, Andrew hated him.

"What if a spirit visited us in our room at night and talked directly to us?" she had once asked Andrew.

"I'd be dreaming."

"What if it was in the light of day in your lab?"

"I'd walk down to the emergency room and sign myself in, because I'd know I was hallucinating."

Regardless, Coco did believe. As she taught the third graders in the Art-in-the-Schools program or worked on the piece she had been invited to create for an April show at the Cultural Center, she conjured up images of Roy. If he couldn't make actual contact with her father, Roy would have insight into the suicide letter. She wanted to drive out to Statesville to see him. She knew Andrew would disapprove, but he would never forbid her. In fact, he would probably rather she drive an icy road out to a prison than become more depressed. And since reading her father's letter, she had felt despondent.

In the classes she taught three afternoons a week, the crunch of the children's scissors biting through heavy construction paper no longer delighted her. Even her own piece—a miniature village made of phone book yellow pages shaped and shellacked into buildings, a park, and winding streets—didn't inspire her any more. What had once seemed an exciting project, finding the right advertisements and phone numbers to adhere to the right structures, now seemed monotonous and obvious. She wanted to talk to Roy, but she didn't think it was right to go to the prison pregnant. Her baby came first. Still, she hoped that if she concentrated hard enough he would simply appear.

When she had visited him at Statesville, and told him how sorry she was to see him cooped up, he had cocked his head and smiled in a way that lifted his heavy cheeks. His face appeared a little distorted through the scratched Plexiglas.

"Coco Bean, please, give me a little credit. Do you think they could keep an expert on astral projection flight behind bars?"

They never would have got him if he had paid his taxes. To think it really came down to death and taxes. Coco had heard the saying many times while growing up. Like so many clichés, the implicit truth of it had eluded her, until that day at Statesville.

* * *

Although her mother and Edge, the midwife, were both coming over early to help Coco prepare for the afternoon shower, she started cleaning as soon as she got up. Her mother was a bit of a clean freak. The state of the apartment would upset her. Dust coated surfaces, cobwebs laced corners, and dishes crowded both the kitchen sink and counters. Books and DVDs seldom made their way back to the shelves. Heavy phone books and scraps of thin yellow paper littered the living room floor. On the coffee table, the little yellow city rose from the plywood platform where it had precariously sat for the last three months, like a town seen from an airplane. She and Andrew lived in what they considered a happy chaos, though they knew others might call it a mess.

As she worked, stretching to dust and bending to sweep, the baby seemed to do somersaults. Coco kept calling Andrew from his chores to feel the movement.

"Sounds like he's getting a little claustrophobic," said Andrew, his warm hand on her belly. To be fair, they alternated pronouns, calling the baby "she" one week, "he" the next. They wanted the gender to be a surprise. "Maybe you should just take it easy."

"No, the baby is just excited about the gifts," said Coco. "I've got to get this place in shape."

"It doesn't need to be perfect. It's snowing so hard that half the people probably won't even show."

"I'm not trying for perfect, just presentable," said Coco, imagining her mother's lips pulled tight in disapproval. As a widow of a suicide, why wouldn't she always be expecting the worst? "Help me carry the city into the bedroom."

They each took an end of the plywood foundation and—Andrew walking backwards—carried the city, like a big wedding cake on a platter, dipping from side to side, into the bedroom. For months the project had captivated her. Everything seemed to fall into place organically, almost magically, as she worked. Now, as the city teetered between them, it looked like nothing more than a mess of old yellow paper, just a blur of yellow and black. How could she ever fix it? She thought of starting a new piece on suicide notes, but she didn't have a firm concept—besides, the project would probably depress her more. She had never been so stuck like this on a piece.

"Should we put it on the bed?" asked Andrew.

"No, we'll need that for coats," said Coco. "How about between the bed and the window? I think there's enough room."

As she knelt down, the baby bucked; a cramp soared up her side.

"You know, I think you're right. I will rest for a little while."

* * *

Edge was the first guest to arrive, carrying loaves of ginger-bread wrapped in sheets of aluminum foil crinkly from a hundred previous uses. Edge had been a friend of her mother's, and the owner of the home day care center Coco had attended as a child.

Though Edge had lost touch with Coco's mother, Coco had always thought lovingly of Edge. As a very young child she had literally thought of Edge as *the woman in the shoe who had so many children that she didn't know what to do*. Coco's mother ran into Edge at the beginning of Coco's pregnancy and learned that she had given up the day care center when her last child left home. Since then, she had trained as a midwife. Though Coco had an obstetrician, it seemed only natural that she would work with Edge as well, visiting her every few weeks for advice on nutrition and birthing. Now Edge resembled the woman in the nursery rhyme more than ever. In addition to her own five children, she had four grandchildren who were often at her house when Coco came for her appointments. Edge had aged gracefully. Her jawline was still firm and her white hair flowed to her waist where it blended into brunette tips.

"It's really coming down out there," said Edge as she stomped her high-laced, booted feet in the front hall and handed Andrew the bread, placing her baby gift, wrapped in newspaper from the colored comic strips section, on the chair by the door.

Coco's mother arrived next, followed by Coco's college room-mate, Vicky, and Vicky's latest boyfriend. After that, the stream of guests was so steady that the thoughts of her father and Roy that had dominated Coco's mind for the last few weeks receded into a hazy part of her consciousness. So she was almost surprised when she opened the door to find her Uncle Danny, clasping a shopping bag.

"I brought these old family photo albums for you," said Danny, lifting the bag he was holding to indicate they were inside. "Your Aunt Catherine had them. I'll just put them over there, and you can look at them later. I thought you'd like some baby pictures of your father."

At the beginning of the party, Coco was cautious, waiting for something to go wrong, for awkwardness from bringing together people from different parts of her life, for her mother to be uncomfortable around Daniel, for Andrew's colleagues to be unable to talk to her family or friends. Yet, to her surprise, people slowly mingled. Within the first thirty minutes, the party actually became fun. It was as if no one in the room had anything else in the world more important to do than watch her open baby gifts and eat gingerbread; the blizzard had bound everyone together, making the desire to leave and get on the snow-covered roads less attractive. The guests seemed happy in the warm cocoon of the apartment she shared with Andrew. Coco was enjoying herself so much that she didn't tell anyone when her water broke in the bathroom. She simply soaked it up with a large towel and changed her pants. Nor did she mention her first contraction. She didn't want to stop watching Andrew's amazement over the size of the infant clothes being unwrapped, nor her mother chatting merrily with Danny as if they hadn't been estranged for more than twenty years. It was so rare that Coco saw her mother happy. Laughter and music and Edge pouring wine.

When all the food had been eaten and the gifts unwrapped, there were parting kisses and promises to call soon. It was dark outside and still snowing. Big thick white flakes like torn paper fluttering down from the heavens. When only Andrew, her mother, and Edge were left, removing plates and stuffing discarded wrapping paper into trash bags, Coco sank into their one armchair and announced her condition.

"I think the baby is coming. I've been having contractions for a while, most of the shower in fact."

Andrew spun around.

"Why didn't you say something?" he asked.

"How far apart?" asked Edge, holding up her hand to silence Andrew.

"I'd guess about five minutes now," said Coco.

"Five minutes? And they only started at the beginning of the shower? It's coming fast, faster than usual for a first baby. We can still make it to the hospital. The main roads will be clear."

"No," said Coco. "I want to have it here, at home."

"But, Coco, honey, what if something goes wrong?" asked Yolunda. "And a hospital is so much cleaner."

"Cleanliness is overrated," said Edge. "A little dust and dirt does an infant good, builds up the immune system."

"Coco, is this really what you want?" asked Andrew.

What felt like two huge hands inside Coco's belly squeezed and pushed down on the baby.

"Yes, and I think the baby wants to be born here, too. We have a midwife and a nurse. What more could we possibly need? The baby *has* to come out. There's no choice."

Andrew's whisker-like scars blushed. He turned to Edge and asked, "So what do we need to do to get ready?"

Yolunda sighed and said, "I'll start on the bedroom."

As Edge issued instructions to Andrew, Coco slid farther down in the armchair and panted.

* * *

When Coco felt the hard head emerge between her thighs, the voices surrounding her grew distant. It was as if she had become enveloped in a thick and moist bubble made from sweat and fluids. Dim voices called to her from the other side, *PUSH*, and she pushed. Flesh tingling, the space between her legs widened so that she could feel the roundness of the skull and imagine the baby's ears scrunched tightly against the head like miniature morning glories ready to burst open with the light. *PUSH*, a chorus called from beyond. Then, a solitary word, *BREATHE*, came from what sounded like Edge. *Breathe*—Coco had never considered the word quite this way. *Breathe*, the gentle way to move the air. In a synaptic flicker, Coco saw an image of her father: alone in his studio, a gun in his right hand—the same long-fingered hand she could still picture in her mind's eye from her childhood. It was the first time he had appeared since she and Roy last had sex. Coco felt scared. She squeezed her eyes to block out the image. *BREATHE. BREATHE.* Her father, she told herself, had not—as he had claimed in his final letter—selected the only way. He was not moving the air by pulling the trigger—he was stopping it. Coco thought of the children in her art class, snapping the air with their scissors; she thought of moving her breath through her body in yoga; she even thought of Roy soaring through the air in real or imagined astral flight. These were the images she wanted to cling to. If only her father had looked, he would have seen that there were many ways to move the air. She pushed, and pictured her miniature yellow city. The concept wouldn't be ruined if she added a little color, just faint crayon lines and circles in key places. Perhaps a fan to make the paper flutter, to send a breeze through the city.

Pain seared her spine and she wrenched back into the moment. As she panted, trying to reduce the pain, Coco couldn't believe her mind had drifted to her work, her art, at such a time. Was she really so like her father? *PUSH. PUSH IT OUT.* Coco realized that was what scared her—she was afraid she was like her father, afraid that she would end the same way. *PUSH. JUST ONE MORE TIME.*

She was like her mother, too. Her mother had known life was a fight, would always be a fight, yet she had been able to keep moving forward, for herself and for her daughter. Coco bore down with all her strength.

BREATHE. How she moved the air was her decision.

An avalanche gave way inside Coco.

"Oh, my God, look, it's here!" said Andrew, his voice sounding watery and remote.

Coco heard a cry, cat-like at first, struggling, against mucus and surprise, to find air before breaking into a full and hungry wail.

Chicago Tribune

Birth Announcements
December 17, 2008

Jasmine Ayre Fulton, 7 pounds, 14 ounces, was born to Coco Doyle and Andrew Fulton at 2 a.m. on December 14.

About the Author

Garnett Kilberg Cohen's awards include the Lawrence Foundation Prize from *Michigan Quarterly Review*, the *Crazyhorse* Fiction
Prize, and four awards from the Illinois Council of the Arts. Her
first story collection, *Lost Women, Banished Souls*, was published by
the University of Missouri Press. Her writing has appeared in many
publications, including *American Fiction, Ontario Review, The An-
tioch Review, The Literary Review,* and *Other Voices*. She teaches at
Columbia College Chicago.

Other Recent Titles from Mayapple Press:

Geof Hewitt, *The Perfect Heart: Selected & New Poems*, 2010
        Paper, 110 pp, $16.95 plus s&h
        ISBN 978-0932412-928

Don Cellini, *Translate into English*, 2010
        Paper, 70 pp, $14.95 plus s&h
        ISBN 978-0932412-911

Susan Slaviero, *Cyborgia*, 2010
        Paper, 78 pp, $14.95 plus s&h
        ISBN 978-0932412-904

Myra Sklarew, *Harmless*, 2010
        Paper, 92 pp, $15.95 plus s&h
        ISBN 978-0932412-898

William Heyen, *The Angel Voices*, 2010
        Paper, 66 pp, $14.95 plus s&h
        ISBN 978-0932412-881

Robin Chapman and Jeri McCormick, eds, *Love Over 60: an anthology of women's poems*, 2010
        Paper, 124 pp, $16.95 plus s&h
        ISBN 978-0932412-874

Betsy Johnson-Miller, *Rain When You Want Rain*, 2010
        Paper, 74 pp, $14.95 plus s&h
        ISBN 978-0932412-867

Geraldine Zetzel, *Mapping the Sands*, 2010
        Paper, 76 pp, $14.95 plus s&h
        ISBN 978-0932412-850

Penelope Scambly Schott, *Six Lips*, 2010
        Paper, 88 pp, $15.95 plus s&h
        ISBN 978-0932412-843

Toni Mergentime Levi, *Watching Mother Disappear*, 2009
        Paper, 90 pp, $15.95 plus s&h
        ISBN 978-0932412-836

Conrad Hilberry and Jane Hilberry, *This Awkward Art*, 2009
        Paper, 58 pp, $13.95 plus s&h
        ISBN 978-0932412-829

Chris Green, *Epiphany School*, 2009
        Paper, 66 pp, $14.95 plus s&h
        ISBN 978-0932412-805

For a complete catalog of Mayapple Press publications, please visit our website at *www.mayapplepress.com*. Books can be ordered direct from our website with secure on-line payment using PayPal, or by mail (check or money order). Or order through your local bookseller.